A Place In The Sun

Books by Lewis Warsh

POETRY

The Suicide Rates
Highjacking
Moving Through Air
Chicago (with Tom Clark)
Dreaming As One
Long Distance
Immediate Surrounding
Blue Heaven
Hives
Methods of Birth Control
The Corset
Information From the Surface of Venus
Avenue of Escape
Private Agenda (with Pamela Lawton)
The Origin of the World
Debtor's Prison (with Julie Harrison)
Reported Missing
The Flea Market in Kiel
Flight Test
Inseparable: Poems 1995–2005
Donatello
Alien Abduction
Out of the Question: Poems 1963-2003

FICTION

Agnes & Sally
A Free Man
Money Under The Table
Touch Of The Whip
Ted's Favorite Skirt
A Place In The Sun
One Foot Out the Door: Collected Stories

AUTOBIOGRAPHY

Part Of My History
The Maharajah's Son
Bustin's Island '68

TRANSLATION

Night Of Loveless Nights by Robert Desnos

EDITOR

The Angel Hair Anthology (with Anne Waldman)

A PLACE IN THE SUN

Lewis Warsh

Spuyten Duyvil
New York City

Sections of this book first appeared in *Conjunctions*, *The Brooklyn Rail*, *The Metro Times*, and in the anthology *Here Lies* (2001). Thanks to Bradford Morrow, Tod Thilleman, Donald Breckenridge, Katt Lissard, George Tysh, Karl Roeseler, Gil Ott, and Wang Ping.

copyright © 2010 Lewis Warsh

ISBN 978-1-933132-71-6

Cover art by Pamela Lawton

Library of Congress Cataloging-in-Publication Data

Warsh, Lewis.
A place in the sun / Lewis Warsh.
p. cm.
ISBN 978-1-933132-71-6
I. Title.
PS3573.A782P56 2009
813'.54--dc22

2009026427

CONTENTS

The Russians

Secret

A Place in the Sun

Mysterioso

Endless Embrace

Harry Cray

for Monty & Liz

THE RUSSIANS

The two Russian women were in the kitchen of their apartment when Eddie Perez came in through the window with a gun. One of the women, her blue eyes shielded by tiny gold-rimmed glasses, was standing in front of an ironing board in her underwear. It was ninety degrees outside, hotter inside the apartment. The other woman was sitting at the kitchen table with her back to the window drinking coffee. The two women were in their early twenties. Marina, the woman in the nightgown at the table, had emigrated to the United States five years before. The other woman, in bra and panties at the ironing board, had arrived several months ago. They had been friends in Odessa; now they were roommates in New York City. It had been Marina's job, since she had studied English at the university in Odessa and could speak English fluently, to come to the United States first and find an apartment. The plan was for Irene to follow, once she had settled in. The fact that five years passed before she arrived was another story.

The man named Eddie Perez had just killed a policeman in the stairwell of a building in the housing projects on Avenue D. There were at least a hundred policemen in the neighborhood looking for him. He had escaped to the tenement rooftops, even though there was a helicopter overhead, and had climbed down a fire escape along the side of the building where the Russian women shared an apartment on the top floor. The policemen in the street below assumed he was holding someone hostage in the apartment. The two women were slow to react when he came in the window. Irene simply put down her iron and stared at the man with her mouth open, while Marina turned a slow half-circle in her chair, sandwich in hand.

"Don't say anything, not a word," the man said. He rotated the gun, pointing it first at Irene, then at Marina.

One of the policemen, possibly the police commissioner, was shouting up at him through a bullhorn, asking him to surrender. Pleading with him, really. Where before there had been the animated noise of people talking, the rise and fall of distant sirens, now there was silence, nothing but the voice of the cop. He was repeating the same phrase—"Come out with your hands up"—like the refrain of a song echoing down the sides of a canyon.

"Eddie," he was saying, "if you hear this, come out of the building with your hands in the air."

Eddie Perez could hear the cop's words. The whole scene made him want to laugh. He went to the kitchen sink, turned on the cold water, and splashed it over his face. The two women were numb with the heat. He waved his gun in their faces and muttered to himself, interspersing Spanish curse words with English. The two women believed him when he said he would kill them if they didn't follow his instructions. They had learned to anticipate the unexpected in a new country, and now it was happening. A baby-faced young man was pointing a gun at them at eleven o'clock on a morning in August. He had entered their apartment.

"You," he said, pointing to Marina, "give me some tape. And some rope."

He ordered the woman who was wearing only her underwear to lie facedown on the floor. Cops with rifles were stationed on the roof across the street. They were special cops, trained at shooting people from a distance. The guns were aimed at the windows of the apartment where the two Russian women lived. While Irene was on the floor, Eddie Perez strapped Marina to the chair and pasted a strip of masking tape over her mouth.

"Get up," he said to Irene, pulling at her arm with his free hand. "Where's the bedroom?"

It was Marina who told the police what had happened. How the man with the gun entered the apartment and tied her to the chair. How he led her half-naked friend into the bedroom.

There were people in the street who were shouting Eddie's name. "Edd-ie, Edd-ie." There were people leaning out their windows chanting the syllables of his name as if he were a war hero or an astronaut or some athlete who earned ten million dollars a year. There was no love lost between the cops and the residents of Avenue D. Eddie had been born in the projects facing the East River Drive. They considered him a kind of folk-hero for wounding a cop who had caught him robbing a grocery on the Upper East Side a few days before. Nothing wrong with robbing a store in a neighborhood where rich people lived. That's why the cops were looking for him in the first place, and that's why he had to kill one of them in a stairwell on Avenue D.

The cop in charge of the case, Harry Cray, decided to lead a team of men up the stairway and break down the door of the apartment, but first he had to try to coax the bastard into taking responsibility for what he had done. As he stood in the street doing nothing, he sensed that something horrible was happening inside the apartment. The sharpshooters across the street couldn't detect any sign of life. Not even the curtains at the window were moving.

Find someone who can talk to the guy in Spanish. Find his mother.

Marina, tied to the chair, said she heard nothing from behind the bedroom door. She assumed that her friend was being raped. Or that he had killed her first. He had killed one cop, wounded another. What did he have to lose? Too bad for the two Russian women who were sitting innocently in their apartment.

A woman who looked as old as Harry Cray's grandmother stepped forth from the crowd.

"I'm Eddie's mother," she said, in English. "Let me speak to him."

Marina assumed that after he killed Irene he would come out and kill her, as well.

Harry Cray handed Eddie's mother the bullhorn and she shouted into it as if she had been preparing for this moment all her life. Harry could see the air vibrate, as if the woman was breathing underwater. All the cops were crouching like stick figures near their cars. The sunlight was baking the roofs of the cars the color of lava, and Harry Cray could see every drop of sweat on the face of Eddie Perez's mother as she shouted to her son in Spanish.

Harry knew that the words she used wouldn't be strong enough to convince her son to give himself up. Her voice was raspy and hoarse and she kept repeating the word "Dios, Dios" as if that was going to make any difference. Eddie had gone too far this time. And maybe this woman wasn't even Eddie's mother, but someone playing the part in a movie about cops he had rented from a video store years before, or a movie yet to be made, a pilot for a new TV series about detectives and their girlfriends and wives.

It was Marina, of course, after it was over, who filled in the blanks. How when his mother was shouting at him through the bullhorn, Eddie Perez was in the back bedroom with Irene and Marina was in the kitchen, tied to her chair, listening to it all. Her friend crying in the other room and the old woman shouting in the street.

It was her turn next. Marina was certain he would kill both of them.

Harry Cray decided that Eddie Perez's mother was only making things worse. He decided that the best plan was to storm the apartment. The point was to take Eddie alive, if possible, but also to insure the safety of whomever he had taken hostage. No one knew if he was alone in the apartment. No one knew about the two women.

Marina, tied to her chair, knew that her friend was dead. There was a period of maybe thirty seconds where the silence was overwhelming. The silence in the bedroom and the silence outside. Even the helicopter circling the scene seemed to have stalled in midair. And then, Marina told Harry Cray, after it was over, I heard your footsteps on the stairs.

He had seen her face, when he entered the apartment, the strip of tape over her mouth. He had seen her eyes. They said *in there*. They pointed him toward the bedroom door. He had walked past her, followed by five men in uniform, and they had stood on either side of the door. He could feel her watching him, her neck muscles bulging beneath her skin, her taut breasts swelling outward, the sweat pouring down the sides of her face. Her hair was sculpted like braided ivy, the color of fire. There was the moment when he had to make a choice, signaling to one of the cops to knock down the door, while at the same time wanting to comfort the young woman in the chair, to kneel at her feet and untie her hands. Rub them between his own to get the blood flowing.

Irene was dead. Eddie was holding her upright in a corner of the room with a gun pressed to the side of her head. The woman was a half-head taller than Eddie and kept slipping from his grasp like a broken mannequin. Harry couldn't believe that Eddie would use a dead body as a hostage.

"Put the gun down, Eddie" he said. "It's over."

The woman had a vague smile on her face, a streak of blood across her forehead.

"I want out of here," Eddie said, tightening his grip on the dead woman. "Get me a car to the airport."

"No chance," Harry Cray said. "You've seen too many movies. It's over."

"It's never over," Eddie said.

And those were his last words.

It was Marina who warned me about Dimitri's wife. "If Natasha ever finds out you're sleeping with her husband, she'll kill you." I had met Dimitri at a party. Marina had introduced us and I guess she felt partially responsible for what might happen. For what did happen. The last thing she expected was that I'd end up with Dimitri. She had invited me to a million parties and introduced me to a million guys. I was often the only non-Russian woman at the party so I always drew a crowd of potential suitors. It was my bad luck that I should end up with the one guy who was married. Not only that: Natasha's brother was a gangster. One of the new breed of hoodlums who collected protection money from the Russian store owners in Brighton Beach, the neighborhood of choice for the Russian immigrants. If Natasha's brother found out about me and Dimitri, Marina went on, we'd both be dead.

Twice a week, Dimitri visited me in my apartment. The only time we spent a night together was the night we met. Natasha and their three kids were out of town, so it was possible for Dimitri to sleep over at my apartment without anyone finding out. After that night, any time we wanted to see one another, he had to lie to Natasha, who was suspicious by nature and made him account for every moment he was out of the house. It was only a matter of time before she asked her brother Boris to ask one of his flunkies to follow Dimitri when he left work. He had told Natasha that he was taking an English course at one of the ESL schools near Penn Station. He even bought a textbook and did the homework assignments. It was a half-truth, at best, since he wanted to learn English, and was actually improving his English by spending time with me, though we hardly talked at all.

What did we do together? Dimitri wanted to know about all my ex-lovers. Why someone like me wasn't married. I was almost thirty, after all, and by the time Natasha was thirty she already had three children. They had met in college in Odessa, where they were born, and where their grandparents still lived. They had been together ten years. I was the first woman Dimitri had slept with since he met Natasha, or so he said. His first affair.

"What's he like?" Marina asked. We were eating lunch on a bench on the promenade in Brooklyn Heights. We went there every afternoon, weather permitting, on our break.

Marina's boyfriend Ivan was just out of jail, and as a consequence I saw less of her. We still went to parties together. All the Russian guys got drunk and took turns dancing with me. Eventually, one of them would get too drunk and start a fight with the others. Marina danced only with Ivan, who had a bad temper, apparently, and had a fit of jealousy if she even talked to another guy.

"Da," Dimitri said, and I repeated it back to him, "da." He was trying to teach me Russian. What we did together was teach each other things. He told me about Russian history. About the Romanovs. Peter the Great. All the tsars with names like Alexander and Nicholas. He told me about Trotsky and Lenin. And I tried to teach him English, though he knew more English than I knew Russian. Twice a week I took Russian lessons from a retired professor on the Upper West Side, a man in his early seventies whose wife had recently died, and whose daughter—"You remind me of my daughter," he said when we first met—lived in California. We would sit in the living room of his apartment, at a large table facing a window with a view of the Hudson River and the smokestacks on the Jersey shore. He would serve me coffee on a gold tray which he said had belonged to his parents in Odessa. That's where he had grown up. His father, he said, had known Lenin.

"*Kafye*," he said. "And *chay*."

"What does *chay* mean?"

"*Chay* means tea. Repeat after me."

"*Kafye*," I said, "and *chay*."

His name was Roshenko, but he told me to call him Karl. That's what his wife used to call him. She had been a ballerina in Russia, before they came here, but she had broken her leg in a bicycle accident and could no longer dance. She had a dream of opening her own dance school but it had never happened. Before she died, she worked in a bridal shop on 5th Avenue, selling wedding gowns to people who never had to worry about money.

I was in the back seat of a car with two Russians and we were all drunk. Marina was in the front seat with her boyfriend Ivan. It was early summer and the windows on either side were wide open. Ivan, who was driving, shouted something to some black guys in a passing car. They were all talking Russian and the guys in the back were laughing, pointing their fingers at the black guys in the car which had stopped alongside us. Sometimes Marina translated for me but this time she didn't and I wondered, as I often did, whether they were talking about me. We were riding down the Belt Parkway, on our way from a party in the West Village to another party in Brighton Beach, where most of the Russians lived, Marina included. I was taking turns kissing the two guys. One of them lifted my skirt and put his hand between my legs while the other began fumbling, like a young schoolboy, with the buttons of my blouse. Both of them were too drunk to wonder whether I wanted them to touch me or not, and for the moment I lacked the energy to push them away. All I knew about them were that they were friends of Ivan's. He had introduced me to them at the first party but I didn't remember their names.

Marina said that her parents had named her after Marina Tsveteva, the great Russian poet who hung herself because she was too poor to feed her children. Because no one cared about her poetry. Because she didn't care about it herself. Is that the story? Most of the Russians I met could recite poetry by heart. It would happen at every party; someone would get drunk and began reciting Pasternak, a poem that all Russians memorized when they were kids.

We met at school, Marina and I, the private school in Brooklyn Heights where we both taught, mostly white kids with a lot of money and black and Hispanic kids on scholarship. I taught English—*The Great Gatsby, As I Lay Dying, The Grapes of Wrath*—to high school students, and Marina, who was a painter and a collagist, taught art—art history, drawing, introduction to painting. Once a week she and Dimitri attended the same drawing class, that's how they met and that's how (eventually) I met Dimitri. That's how all the trouble started. Marina spoke with an accent. I asked her where she came from and she said "Where do you think?" I had to admit that for a long time I had a crush on her myself, and I think she knew this and was frightened of me (this was my theory) because she had no interest in sleeping with women, or she had an interest (wishful thinking) but refused to admit it.

She told me that she once shared an apartment with a Russian friend on 11th Street and Avenue C and that one morning an escaped convict named Eddie Perez climbed in through the window and held them both hostage and even raped and murdered her friend Irene while Marina, tied to a chair, listened to it all from the other room. She said: "I was having breakfast, Irene was ironing a blouse, when this guy came in the window with a gun in his hand." She said that he threatened to kill them if they didn't do what he said. The cops were downstairs, apparently he had killed a cop earlier in the week, or the same day, I can't remember, and someone— the police commissioner, perhaps—was telling him to surrender, shouting the words through a bullhorn from the sidewalk. "He kept telling us that he had nothing to lose. That he was going to spend the rest of his life in jail. That he had already killed someone and that killing us wouldn't make a difference. I wanted him to choose me, not Irene," Marina said, "but he tied me to a chair instead. He said he was twenty-five, but looked younger, really a kid, with a mop of black hair over his forehead. He pointed the gun at Irene and said, 'You—get inside.' I sat in my chair listening to her crying and the guy telling her to keep quiet. And then," she said, "they were both quiet. And then the cops came and killed him."

After that, she moved to Brighton Beach, where she lived when she first came to the states. It was the only neighborhood where she felt safe.

I want to concentrate on the Russians, what I know, what I learned. Everything you don't learn in school I learned from my relationships with Dimitri and Marina. The only way to learn anything, possibly, is to experience it first hand, this goes without saying. I want to focus on the time I spent with the Russians. I was a California girl, so to speak, though I had been living in New York for five years, escaping a bad marriage back home, bad parents who had split up when I was ten. The phase of my life that involved the Russians only lasted a few years, but whenever someone mentions Odessa, I feel like I've been there.

Something else happened during this time that only indirectly involves my life with the Russians. I still have his name in my address book: Harry Cray. Next to his address there are two numbers, his home phone and the precinct where he worked. Harry Cray was a cop. The woman in the apartment below me, a prostitute named Yvonne de Marco, had been murdered, and late one Sunday night Harry Cray and his partner Ricardo knocked on my door. I had just gotten out of the shower and was wearing the blue terrycloth robe which Dimitri had bought me for Christmas when I heard the footsteps on the staircase, followed by the knock. And in answer to my question: Who is it? one of them—it must have been Harry—said: The cops. It's the cops.

One thing I know about are cops. My father was a cop. My first lover was a cop. There had even been talk, when I was growing up, that I was going to become a cop. I'm an only child—my mother nearly died giving birth to me and didn't want to risk having more kids—and it was the tradition in my father's family that the children follow in their father's footsteps. Every male in my father's line had been a cop since I don't know when. The Civil War maybe. Every son went into the army. My father had been in Vietnam. He was in Vietnam when I was born and didn't hear that my mother almost died giving birth to me until he returned home for a week's leave. I didn't see much of my father when I was growing up. I call him up on his birthday and he calls me on Christmas. He calls me when he knows he's coming to New York, which is about once a year, and we eat dinner together. He says: "You choose a restaurant" and I say "What do you like to eat?" I have almost no memory of sitting around a dinner table with my parents when I was a kid. My mother hated to cook. When my father was in Vietnam my mother took a job as a real estate agent. We were living in a small town along the coast about an hour north of San Francisco. My mother sold houses to rich hippies. She had sex with her boss. She hired a babysitter to take care of me. Every time the phone rang she assumed it was someone from the army informing her that her husband had died in the line of duty or was missing in action. She dreamed that a coffin containing his body parts had been left on the front porch. She told her lover, Joe Griffiths, the real estate mogul who became my stepfather, that it was wishful thinking. "Even if he came back in a wheelchair I wouldn't let him in the front door."

The cops introduced themselves. The tall shifty-eyed one with the chalky complexion who did most of the talking—that was Harry. The smaller, younger guy with the bald spot was Ricardo. Harry, staring at a point a few inches above the top of my head, said that the woman who lived below me had been murdered that morning. A friend of hers who had keys to the apartment discovered the body at four in the afternoon. There was a pause as if they were waiting to see how I would react. The tall guy ("My name is Harry Cray, I'm a detective at the ninth precinct") asked me if I'd been home earlier that morning, or the night before, and if so whether I'd heard any suspicious noises, voices, an argument. Did I know the woman downstairs? This was Ricardo talking.

I shook my head.

"Does that mean 'yes'?" Harry asked.

"It means 'I can't believe it,'" I said.

I told the detectives that I'd been living in the building for two years and that Yvonne was living here when I moved in. They didn't ask me for this information but I thought it was important to give some background before I got to the point. Ricardo nodded and wrote down the information on a pad, or pretended to. He unclipped a cheap ball-point and balanced a small notepad in the palm of his hand. They were both standing up, Harry leaning against the sink, Ricardo against the front door. I was sitting in a chair in my blue robe with my legs crossed, smoking a cigarette.

"Did you know that your neighbor was a prostitute?"

"We said hello on the staircase, that's all. Once she asked if I wanted to come by for coffee but I had to go somewhere else and she said whenever I wanted to just knock on her door. It's something people say who live in the same building without really meaning it and of course I never went. I should have, I guess, or invited her up here. We didn't seem to be on the same schedule. Occasionally I heard music from down below. Jazz. Some uncomplicated sounding mood music that didn't bother me at all."

A few days later I was sitting with Marina on the promenade, eating lunch. I told her about the two cops, the murder of the prostitute/porn star in the apartment below. The way I found out she was a porn star was in the newspaper. The cops on the case—the newspaper didn't use their names—said there were tapes in the apartment, porno movies, and magazines with her pictures in it. Marina, nibbling the edge of her sandwich, seemed distracted, like she was only half-listening. She didn't pick up on the fact that I was interested in the detective, Harry Cray. I didn't even know his name. What I was conveying in the story had nothing to do with Yvonne de Marco, my dead neighbor, or even the porn star angle, but my interest in the cop. Marina was thinking of something else.

"We want to see you again," she said.

I had spent the night—the night Yvonne de Marco was murdered—over at Ivan and Marina's. The three of us had slept together for the first time, Ivan in the middle. At some point he rolled on top of me while Marina leaned on her elbow and watched. When Harry Cray asked whether I'd heard anything in Yvonne's apartment I stared at my feet and said that I wasn't home, that I'd slept over at a friend's house. Harry looked disappointed. I thought he might be jealous since maybe he thought I was saying (indirectly) that I'd slept at my boyfriend's house. That I was unavailable. Was that what I was saying? Or maybe he was disappointed because I hadn't heard anything, that I didn't know anything, that I wasn't going to be any help. Maybe I was just imagining that he was attracted to me but that he was pretending not to be because he was with his partner. Or maybe he was just simply disappointed about being alive, the dwindling possibilities now that he was forty. Was that how old he was? The disappointment in his eyes, along with the deep furrows that rippled across his forehead when he was thinking (what was he thinking about?), made him look older.

It was only in my mind, in a thought that lasted a microsecond, that I imagined I was falling in love. That Harry Cray and I were falling in love. That we'd live together forever. It was the illusion that everything happened by accident and that you had to be prepared for every encounter. That you had to be open to the possibility. Most people walk down the street with their eyes glued to the pavement. No contact, not even a faint possibility. And they complain about being alienated, how New York is such a "lonely place," that you have to protect yourself, that there are too many different types of people, not racial types but people who are brain-damaged, neurotic, schizophrenic, murderous. Angry. There are too many angry people here, that's what everyone thinks. I was angry about something, the defendant explains to his permanently disabled victim, and I took it out on you. That's what people do in the city, they vent their rage on innocent bystanders. They get caught in the crossfire.

I was tempted to tell Marina that I'd only sleep with her and Ivan if she let me have sex with her as well. I hoped that if I went along with her I'd be rewarded for my patience. I wasn't sure what she was getting out of it all, watching me and Ivan from the side of the bed. Looking bored, as if she were just waiting for it to be over. As if she were doing it all ("He's been in jail for six months") for him, to please him. Because she liked the idea of people she loved getting together. Her boyfriend Ivan, and me, her best friend.

"Didn't you have fun the other night?"

Now we had something to talk about.

"And Dimitri. Are you still seeing him?"

She had no interest in hearing about the dead prostitute and the two cops who had come to my apartment.

It was February 1997. Twice a week Dimitri visited me. Once a week I went uptown to see Professor Roshenko. Every other week I spent the night with Marina and Ivan. Dimitri, of course, didn't know I was sleeping with someone else. The Russians are a jealous race, prone to extreme solutions to simple problems, especially when they're drunk. Dimitri always asked me if I had other lovers, couldn't believe that I didn't. I was trying to convince him that it was possible for him to change his life. I was naïve to think that Natasha couldn't force him to stay. Dimitri shook his head. He'd do anything, he said, to get away from her. Even if it meant giving up the kids. She'd never let me have the kids. Then he shook his head again, as if the thought was inconceivable. Marina had once told me that she thought Dimitri was too passive. That was one theory. The other theory was that Natasha had too much power. Whenever there was a murder in Brighton Beach the cops went directly to Natasha's brother. Maybe he had some information? Marina was certain that Natasha's brother was paying off the cops as well.

"If Natasha ever finds out..." Marina shook her head and suggested I carry a gun. Ivan could get one for her, easily. Ivan, a part-time gangster himself, had been arrested for selling drugs out of a storefront on Brighton Avenue. He had been put in jail not so much for the severity of the crime but because he refused to name names, one of whom would be Natasha's brother. When he got out of jail he promised Marina that he would never work for Boris again, but of course it was Boris who had found him his present job, at a print shop in Sheepshead Bay. Nothing illegal about that. The owner of the shop owed Boris a favor, that was all. All the shop owners in Little Odessa, as the Russian neighborhood was called, owed Boris something. The only person to whom Boris owed anything was his sister.

    Professor Roshenko, my Russian teacher, had been with Trotsky in Mexico. There was a framed photograph on his mantelpiece: Trotsky, other members of his staff, a young version of the professor standing next to his hero. Trotsky's hand on his shoulder. Another photograph of Trotsky and Frida Kahlo, another of Trotsky and Diego Rivera, another of the three of them together. Another of Trotsky with his wife Natalia. It was like a little shrine. One of the brightest moments in my life, the professor said. Especially when the trials began. Stalin had indicted Trotsky and it was up to Trotsky to respond, long distance. Every newspaper in the world carried the story. It was Professor Roshenko's job to talk to reporters. We worked for eighteen hours a day. We had one focus, one goal. Except for the early years with my wife, this was the most exciting time for me.

    The next time Dimitri and I had sex I thought of Harry Cray. What we would do together if he came to my apartment alone to ask me more questions (this was his excuse for visiting me) about the dead porn star downstairs. Of course I never told Dimitri that when I was having sex with him I was thinking of someone else. Thinking about something is the same as doing it. According to St. Augustine, thoughts are as sinful as actions. The only way I can come when I'm making love is to imagine that I'm making love to someone else. There's a knock on my apartment door and the voice says: It's the police. I remember him, of course, from the other day, when he came by with his partner Ricardo. One might imagine making love to both Harry and his partner simultaneously—I've never had sex with two guys at the same time—as Yvonne de Marco did in all her movies. And then after they were done there were two more guys, it went on forever, until the cocks moving in and out of her body resembled the pistons in a car, close-up of a car's inner workings, a training film for fledgling auto mechanics: this is how it's done.

One afternoon, on our lunch break, Marina told me she thought that Ivan was falling in love with me. She said that Ivan, who wanted to be a film director, was writing a film script and had told Marina that I would be perfect for the lead role. They invited me over for dinner and we watched movies together in the living room. Me and Marina on the living room rug, her head on my stomach, while Ivan sat in a chair close to the screen. Often we watched movies that Ivan had seen before. He was writing the script for a movie and was planning to send it to a movie producer named Dean Holmstrom whom he had met through Boris. He was in Boris's good graces ever since he went to jail without incriminating anyone. He had served his time, without complaining, and this was his reward.

He told us of a party he went to at Dean Holmstrom's house. Elizabeth Taylor had been there. She had just come out of the hospital and spent most of the time sitting in a chair in the corner. Everyone at the party paid homage to her. Everyone at the party was aware that she was there. Ivan was amazed at her body, especially her breasts. He had expected her to be heavyset and somewhat grotesque. It was easy to see how she had often been described as "the most beautiful woman in the world." When he went to shake her hand, or kiss her hand, she leaned forward so that he could see down the front of her dress. It was a very low-cut evening gown, ankle-length, since her legs were the least attractive part of her body. It was like being in the room with some ancient deity. Something to tell your grandchildren.

Apparently, Dean Holmstrom's wife had given him a tour of the house, a brownstone in the east sixties. She asked him about his script and he told her it was about two Russian women who came to New York and what happened. She promised him more than once that she would make sure Dean read it.

"Did you sleep with her?" Marina asked. It was hard to know from her tone whether she was serious or not and for a moment I wasn't sure who she was referring to. Elizabeth Taylor? The director's wife?

I was worried what would happen to our friendship if I continued to have sex with Ivan. The unspoken rule was that we would never get together when she wasn't around. Sometimes he called me in the evenings and made me promise never to tell her that we had talked. What he wanted to tell me about was his script. It was based on the Eddie Perez story. The guy who had killed the two cops as well as Marina's friend Irene. He wanted me to play Irene. Marina, of course, would play herself. He was thinking of us when he was writing even though I wasn't Russian. He was waiting to hear from Dean Holmstrom. He had left a first draft of the script at his house the night of the party where he had met Elizabeth Taylor.

Marina and I no longer ate lunch together every day. She had too much work, she said, but I didn't believe her. Instead, she ate her lunch in her small office at school. I didn't know how long she could endure the idea that I was sleeping with her lover. She had thought that anything was possible, that she would do anything to make Ivan happy, but the way I saw it she was getting burned by her own fire. Ivan told me on the phone that he and Marina were no longer having sex. He asked me whether I was seeing someone else and I lied, I said "no," even though it seemed possible that Marina had already told him I was sleeping with Dimitri. The only time Marina and I talked these days was when she called to make arrangements for me to come over. When I complained—"I never see you anymore"—she apologized and said that she was busy. I wanted to ask her whether she and Ivan were having problems. I wanted to tell her that I was in love with her, that it was her I wanted to sleep with, not Ivan, but

I didn't say anything. "Can you come over Friday?" And then silence, as if she wanted to get off the phone. As if someone was listening on the other end

Sometimes Dimitri called to cancel our appointment.

"I can't make it," he said. "I'm sorry."

I was getting sick of the deception that involved having an affair with him, but it was too late. I'd had an affair with a married man once before, one of my professors in college (when I was in California), and it had ended badly. Dimitri was in love with me, or so he said. Whenever I acted distant he promised to leave Natasha. "I can't live without you," he would say. He didn't have to tell me why he couldn't come over. It was understood that it had something to do with Natasha. The Russians lived in a small community, everyone knew everyone else's business, and I assumed it was just a matter of time before Natasha found out that I was sleeping with her husband, or that Dimitri found out that I was sleeping with Ivan.

I assumed that Ivan knew about Dimitri and that he didn't care. He had no right to care. If he wanted to cause trouble, if his jealousy took the upper hand, he could make sure that Natasha found out that her husband was having an affair, and with whom. I could imagine a scenario in the future where Ivan felt possessive about me as well. "I want to leave Marina and be with you," I could hear him say.

I guess you could say that a good part of my life involved my dealings with the Russians. I was sleeping with two Russian men, Dimitri and Ivan. My best friend was Russian. Twice a week I went uptown to Professor Roshenko's apartment where I studied Russian, talked to him in Russian, converted my thoughts into a different language. In my spare time I read books in English by Russian writers. I watched Russian movies. My favorite Russian movie was *Solaris,* a science fiction movie about people on a spaceship whose memories are somehow encapsulated by the ocean, enabling people who are dead to return to life. It was a beautiful, languorous movie, that was also a love story. The person who returned by way of the ocean knew he or she was dead. The movie was filled with longing for something that was lost. When I told Ivan that I liked *Solaris* he asked me if I'd seen other movies by Tarkofsky and when I said that I hadn't he said he would get a different one and that we could all watch it the next time I came over.

It was early April and I had begun thinking that when summer came I would change my life. I would stop seeing Dimitri. I would extricate myself from the relationship with Ivan. I would travel to California or to Mexico and when I returned to New York I would change jobs so that I wouldn't have to see Marina everyday. I had studied enough Russian that if I ever decided to go there I could engage in simple conversations. When I was in Brighton Beach I always impressed myself by being able to read the odd-looking lettering on the canopies and windows of the shops. I had wanted to recreate my own identity as a way of getting closer to Marina. But I didn't want to be her sister, that wasn't the point, and it was no longer possible to deny what I was really feeling. It occurred to me that I wouldn't be unhappy if I never saw any of these people again.

Marina felt grateful to Harry Cray for saving her life. After the Eddie Perez incident, after she moved to her own apartment in Brighton Beach, they talked on the phone once or twice a week and occasionally went out for dinner together. She asked him questions about his life, about his marriage, why it had ended, why he had decided to become a cop, how he felt when he'd entered the apartment and saw her sitting in the chair, what it felt like to kill someone. She had thought, more than once, of returning to Russia after Irene was murdered, at least for a visit, until her boyfriend Ivan was released from jail, but she decided that moving in a backward direction was a way of admitting defeat.

"I'll make dinner for you," she told Harry over the phone. She gave him directions to her apartment, a one-bedroom in a building near the ocean.

She wanted to have sex with him as a way of repaying him for saving her life. She thought that it might be possible to sleep with him a few times, not get involved, really, make it clear to him that she was involved with someone else, but that she felt drawn to him because of what he had done. She knew that once they had sex it would be difficult to extricate herself from the relationship after Ivan returned. It was hard to gauge another person's feelings, especially after you made love to them, how everything changed once that happened, but the fact that you couldn't predict what might happen was what made it exciting in the first place. She felt drawn to Harry Cray, to the sense of danger surrounding him, and to the fact that he had never showed any interest in having sex with her, that he treated her more like a daughter than a potential lover. He gave her the impression, though he was over forty, that he hadn't had much experience with women.

They were sitting on the small sofa in her living room looking through photograph albums. She showed him a photograph of Irene, the day they graduated from the university in Odessa. She told him that Irene had had a baby when she was eighteen, that the baby had died when he was six months, but that otherwise Irene had been one of the happiest people she had ever known. As she talked she put her hand on Harry Cray's knee, wanting him to respond. They were sitting very close together on the sofa, their thighs touching. She thought that if she touched him first he would take the cue that he could do anything he wanted with her, that she would let him do anything. She kept her hand on his thigh as he turned the pages of the photo album.

She was frightened that if she acted too aggressively he would leave. It had been three months since her friend had been murdered and she was still in a state of shock. She had never slept with an American before. It was interesting the way feeling gratitude toward someone translated into a feeling of love. Harry Cray wasn't her type, really, she wasn't fixated on older men. She felt like she wanted to give him something, that he needed something, but she wasn't sure what. It was hard for her to imagine that he wouldn't want to make love to her. She had never had any trouble attracting men.

He was lying on his back on the sofa and she was kneeling on the floor, her head between his legs. She unfastened the buckle of his belt and pulled his pants down along his thighs. She was wearing an old Indian skirt with bells on the hem which she had bought at the Salvation Army. A string of beads extended down to her waist. She had the feeling that Harry Cray might come too quickly if she continued and she wanted him inside her. Her hair hung down the side of her face and brushed against his skin. She lifted her blouse and he reached out and put his hand on her breast. She had the feeling that he hadn't made love to anyone in a long time. She thought that she might get pregnant if he came inside her but she would take her chances.

After the first time he became more aggressive. She was making it easy for him. Lying on the living room carpet, pulling him down on top of her. She said something in Russian to him that meant "go slowly" and he said "What? What did you say?" and she remembered that she wasn't making love to Ivan and she didn't bother translating as he went for her hair, tugging at it gently at first and then harder as they exchanged places and she climbed on top of him. So this was what he was like, really, this was the danger. This was what a guy who could murder someone was like in bed. This was where gratitude ended: she was on her knees and he was coming at her from behind. He was remembering what it was like during the first years with his wife when they made love every night in a different position. Everything he knew about sex he had learned from his wife Sara, who was a few years older than he was and infinitely more experienced. Marina thought of saying "You can hit me if you want" because it occurred to her that that's what he wanted to do without realizing it. She wanted to do something with him that he had never done before, that would be a real gift, something for him to remember. She didn't want to come, not yet, his tongue moving between her legs. He was holding her by the waist, her skirt bunched up around her hips, then pulling her hair, then leaning forward to bite the side of her neck. She was glad that she was seeing this part of him and that the feeling of gratitude was what made it possible. He had risked his life for her and she would do anything in return. He had come inside her twice. It was almost midnight and she was going down on him again.

She asked him if he wanted something to drink and she brought him a glass of water. She turned her back to him and he put his arm around her waist and she lifted her leg so that he could come inside her. Then he rubbed her clitoris again, moving slowly, so that he was doing two things at once like Sara had taught him. She began to make noises, breathing heavily, in a way that Sara had done during the first years of their marriage when they had sex, when it seemed like all the energy in her life was directed toward pleasing him. He would return home from work exhausted and she would draw him into the bedroom. "I've been waiting for this all day," she would say. Her appetite for sex had worried him but it was only because he was too inexperienced to understand that this was what he wanted to do as well. Instead, he took her for granted, assumed that she would be there when he came home, that she would always want to have sex with the same intensity, that if he asked her for something she would get it for him. It never occurred to him that she was unsatisfied playing the role of the cop's wife, that she hated lying in bed at night not knowing when he would come home. He always called her if he was coming home late but when the phone rang in the middle of the night she was sure it was someone calling to tell her that he'd been killed or injured. It never occurred to him that she might have a lover during the time when he was at work. He never asked himself what she did when he was at work and Veronica was in school. When he returned home in the middle of the night—not dead, not injured, but what difference did it make?—she turned away from him when he got into bed. "I'm tired," she said, "let's do it tomorrow." It never occurred to him that she had spent the day in bed with someone else and that she was too tired to have sex again.

Marina said, "Don't move—just relax—let me do the work." She wasn't quite sure he understood what she meant. It wasn't the first time she had said this to someone. It was three in the morning. She knelt at his feet at the end of the bed. She took his toes in her mouth, one at a time. "Don't do that," he said. She licked the soles of his feet. "I want to," she said. "Let me."

It took a long time. The only part of him she didn't kiss was his cock. He put his hand out to touch her breast but she pushed him away. It was almost morning. She was on top of him again as the light came in through the curtains. Her cunt was sore, her hair matted with sweat, and she wondered whether he could come again, how long it would go on. She was already thinking of the future, what she would say to him when he called. She sat on a corner of the bed and she touched herself while he watched. There's a mirror at the end of the bed and he can watch himself fucking her from behind, can see her face. They look like people in a funhouse, distorted, a monster with four arms and two heads. They look like the same person. He watched her in the mirror as she knelt on the edge of the bed. She kissed his ankles and his knees. She made a circle with her tongue around his cock without touching it.

"We can do this every night," she says. She doesn't know why she says it. Maybe for a few nights, at best. She had the thought that Ivan had hired someone to watch her, to make sure she didn't sleep with anyone else when he was in prison. He would be out in a few months. Every weekend she visited him, taking the train upstate. He said, "write to me about sex, tell me what you want to do." All he wanted was to talk to her about sex.

She's thinking in Russian. She wonders about Harry Cray's gun. She asks him about it. "I'd like to see it," she says. It was always possible that someone was spying on her and that Harry would be murdered as a consequence. That no one, least of all Ivan, would realize that her lover was a cop. And she would die too. They would kill them both when they were in bed. She had seen it in the movies. The door opens, the man with the machine gun, the unsuspecting lovers, the bullet holes, the screams. The idea of the danger involved is what made her excited and why she asked him to show her the gun. She would do anything in gratitude for saving her life. She wondered what he would think if he knew her boyfriend was in prison.

It's Sunday. Neither of them has to be anywhere. Today is the day that she visits Ivan in jail. He'll be expecting her. His family is in Russia and she's the only person who visits him. Harry takes her hand and places it on his cock. It's almost noon and she gets excited thinking about making love to Ivan. They sit up in bed smoking cigarettes. Harry says that he quit a few years ago but he can't resist the temptation. He draws the smoke into his lungs and then reaches across her for the glass of water on the bedside table. He remembers sex and cigarettes with Sara in the early days of their marriage and then he remembers seeing Sara walking in front of him down the street with another man, their arms around each other's waists. It was in the last months of their marriage. The last weeks and days.

"Did you come?" he asks. He isn't sure. It's like a long thread, now, almost continuous, from one orgasm to another. She doesn't want him to stop. She says, "You have to tell me what you want me to do." She begins with his toes, his ankles, his knees, his hipbone, his nipples. She thinks that if she continues he'll come without her touching him but he doesn't and finally he yanks at her hair and pulls her on top of him. He feels tempted to slap her across the face, but doesn't. He wants to go farther inside her, to regain control, so he pushes her on her side. She wonders why he doesn't take his belt from his pants and use it on her like a whip. She gets wet just thinking about it and watches them in the mirror as he pushes against her until she no longer recognizes herself. Then she sees it, the way she looked when she was thirteen or fifteen, when she was still a virgin. That's how she feels now as he comes inside her.

He takes out his gun and presses it against the side of her head. They're lying back on the bed. It's midafternoon. There are no bullets in the gun, at least that's what he tells her. "I was only kidding," she said, not knowing whether he was about to turn into a monster. She took the gun in her hand and pointed it at their reflections in the mirror. All she knew was that she never wanted to see him again. She wanted to let it go. Either that or they'd have to stay like this indefinitely. Every time he moved away she grabbed his hand and placed it between her legs. She wondered how often he could come. Twice an hour? There was always the chance that one of Ivan's friends was waiting in the street. She sensed that he was falling in love with her, that he had fallen in love with her the first time he saw her sitting in the chair. He took the gun from her hand and placed it on the floor at the side of the bed. He reached out and touched her cheek, a moment of tenderness as she moved on top of him. She taught him how to touch her clitoris when they were fucking, to put his hand between their bodies. She thought it might be possible for them to come at the same time, but it didn't matter. They were in the shower and she was on her knees again with his cock in her mouth. She was bending over so that he could enter her from behind, but it was hard for them to fit. He kept slipping out. He soaped her back, her cunt, put his fingers inside her.

He wanted to ask her if he could spend the night. Possibly they could get something to eat? She was already wondering if she would have to move. She could imagine coming home late at night and Harry would be waiting for her outside her building. Or he would see her with Ivan and know that her boyfriend was a criminal. You can always tell, Ivan once said, whether a person's been in jail or not. Eventually there would be a confrontation. She was grateful to Harry Cray for saving her life but she didn't want anyone else to die. Irene had died. Eddie

Perez had cut her throat. Then Harry Cray shot Eddie through the head. Wasn't that enough?

In the photographs they looked like any other teenage girls. They had their arms around each other, or one of them was behind the other with her head resting on the other's shoulder. Marina was taller so she was often the one who was standing behind Irene. They were inseparable. They were virgins. At fifteen—the time the photo was taken—they had yet to fall in love.

Things began to change when they went to the university in Odessa. Irene was always a bit more advanced than Marina in her relationships with men. She had an agenda which included friendship, but there was something else. There was an older man who lived alone around the corner from where she lived with her parents. In his early forties. Irene, at the time, was only seventeen. She began to visit him once or twice a week after school. He had some physical disability, a back problem, that prevented him from working. He did some kind of paperwork for money at his desk. He rarely went out and Irene would bring him food that he liked and even cooked it for him at times. It was at this point that Irene and Marina began to drift apart. Irene's life with the older man was a secret. If her parents ever found out they would kill her. And him too.

It was after Irene became pregnant that things began

to change. She moved away from her parents without telling them she was going to have a baby. There was a rumor that her parents knew she was pregnant and asked her to leave. The only person she told was Marina, who was shocked at first, since she had yet to have a lover of her own. She had a different goal: to get out of Odessa, out of Russia. She had decided when she was in high school that she wanted to live in the United States and was studying English so when the moment came she would be ready. That's what she did at night, she sat alone with her books. The only person who mattered to her was Irene, her friend from high school. When Irene came to her dormitory room and told her she was pregnant, Marina asked "With who?" It seemed like the logical question. "Who's the father?" Irene told her about how she had been spending her weekday afternoons, in bed with the older man with the back injury. A man with scars who didn't know he was about to become a father.

They lived together in a one-room apartment not far from the university. Marina had a desk near the window where she did her schoolwork late into the night. Irene had dropped out of school when she learned she was pregnant. There was only one bed and the two young women slept together. Marina tried to deny to herself that she was in love with Irene. It was not something she wanted to think about. She had many men who were interested in her and occasionally she went out on dates with them and allowed them to buy her things. She would press her face against the window of a store and exclaim how much she wanted a particular object, and the man she was with would buy it for her in the hope that she would want to sleep with him, but she never did.

The apartment was badly heated and sometimes Irene and Marina slept in each other's arms for warmth. They would fall asleep on separate sides of the bed and wake up, embarrassed, with their arms around each other.

The baby, a boy named Sasha, was born prematurely, and died when he was six months old. Irene tried to nurse him but he cried incessantly. He was too small, more like an object you could fit into the palm of your hand than a living thing. He cried and slept and grew thinner. Reddish spots the size of dimes appeared on his cheeks. He sweated constantly. Irene refused to sleep and the doctor insisted that she was contributing to the problem, that she was transferring her anxiety to the baby, that was why the baby wouldn't nurse. "You mean it's my fault that this is happening?" she wailed at the doctor. Marina woke up in the middle of the night and tried to coax her friend into the bed. She was sitting on the floor at the foot of the crib. "It's all my fault," she was saying. It was practically the only thing she ever said. The older man with the scars didn't know that he had fathered a child. He stood at the window of his room waiting for Irene to appear around the corner and wave to him like she had done before, but she never came.

It was after the baby died that Marina and Irene became lovers. They would spend the entire day in bed studying English, memorizing words and phrases in

English, drinking pots of black tea, smoking cigarettes, their long legs intertwined under the blankets and sheets. They would sleep on their backs with their hands between each other's legs. Irene was amused by the fact that Marina was still a virgin. The older man with the scars, Sasha's father, had not been her first lover. Marina would ask her questions about all her lovers, the men who would pick her up on the way home from school. She would stand on a corner and a car would stop and she would get in. She was only sixteen but looked older if she wore makeup. She was never interested in sleeping with men her own age. Once she even slept with the father of a close friend. She saw him watching her out of the corner of her eye and smiled in a way that communicated to him that she was interested in him as well. She had lost count of her lovers. Marina was jealous; compared to her friend, she had lived a sheltered life. All she had done in her short life, or so it seemed, was sit at a desk in front of a book, translating from one language to another. Even so, it took her about an hour to read a page of English.

Irene would occasionally wake up in the middle of the night and run to the place where Sasha's crib had been, the corner of the room near the window, which now contained a little shrine consisting of cheap candles and a picture of Buddha she had found in a flea market. She would wake up in a cold sweat in the middle of the night and grab for Marina's breasts. She would laugh at anything, a voice on the radio, the way she mispronounced the English phrases, all the English curses like "shit" and "fuck you." Her laughter was like a wave, a tsunami, coming out of nowhere. Anyone who heard her laugh would look at her as if something was wrong. There was a tremor in her voice so it was hard to know whether she was laughing or crying. Her laughter sounded like the cry of the baby who had died.

They made love by the light of a candle at the foot of the bed. They ate black bread and drank tea and cooked old vegetables, pointing to them and addressing them in English as if they were people of different genders until they no longer had to translate the words in their heads. Every other day Marina stood on a line outside a bakery and waited several hours for a loaf of bread. They made plans for the future. They went to the local library and stared at black-and-white photographs of New York City. They assumed there was a future, that this room with its memories of the dead baby would eventually fade, that they would one day parade down a boardwalk near a mythical ocean, named after the Greek god Atlas, and live in a community of people like themselves.

Marina was frightened of leaving her friend alone. The plan was for Irene to move back to her parents' apartment and wait until Marina found an apartment for them in New York. It was one of many possible plans. Sometimes the future resembled an open door; at other times it was like a small room with the walls caving in. The thought of being separate for more than a few days terrified them. They took turns weeping and comforting one another. They had to force themselves to get out of bed, to eat, to make tea, to buy cigarettes. If it was up to Irene, she would spend the whole day in bed with her friend.

They sat on a bench looking out at the Black Sea. They had a favorite café, in the shadow of the Potemkin Monument, where they went to drink coffee in the late afternoon. They stayed up half the night reading in bed. Marina practiced her English skills by reading novels by popular American authors, while Irene read books in Russian: Gogol, Chekhov, Isaac Babel. They wondered if the people they passed on the street knew that they were lovers.

Irene's parents were more sympathetic to her now that she was planning to go to the United States. They assumed that Irene would find an apartment large enough for them as well. They apologized for every infraction, every crime they had committed as a parent. They asked Irene to forgive them for their response to her pregnancy, for not helping her when she needed them. They would get down on their knees and beg for forgiveness if she would help them leave the country. They even began studying English together. They invited Marina to dinner. The plan was for Marina to fly to New York and find an apartment. Everyone gave her the names of people to contact when she arrived. She had an uncle in Brighton Beach where she could stay until she found a job. The uncle, in fact, would give her a job as a waitress in his restaurant, if she wanted. Now that Irene was in safe hands, at least she wouldn't starve when she stayed with her parents, the plan to move to the United States began to gather momentum. A few days before leaving, Marina moved to Irene's parents house and spent her last nights in Russia in Irene's narrow bed. The parents wandered around the apartment oblivious to what was really going on. They assumed that Marina was sleeping on a mattress on the floor.

Marina met Ivan in the restaurant under the el, her uncle's restaurant where the local gangsters congregated after hours. She had been in New York for three months already and still lived with her uncle, in a kind of basement apartment beneath the apartment where he lived with his family. As part of the agreement—that he would give her a job in the restaurant, that he would help her find her own apartment, that he would buy her clothing—she had to have sex with him whenever he wanted. She had realized this on the trip from the airport when he took her hand and placed it on his thigh as he drove. "I'll help you," he said, later that night, "if you do something for me." As he talked, he made a hissing sound in the space between his front teeth. His fingertips were stained with tobacco and his beard scraped her face when he pushed himself against her. She never told him that she was still a virgin and she doubted that he even noticed. Marina thought of Irene while they were having sex and some warmth spilled over, spilled out of her, in a sense, and her uncle imagined that he was giving her pleasure. His wife, he complained, refused to make love to him; she had discovered him in bed with another woman a year before and had denied him any pleasure ever since. Forced him to sleep on the couch. "That's where I'm going when I leave here," he said. "The fucking couch."

It was Ivan who saved her, who took her away from her life in the basement. Of course it was necessary to sleep with him as well, to use him in this way in order to make her escape. She had the feeling that Ivan paid her uncle money as a way of releasing her from her obligation. It was a kind of servitude, either way, but Ivan was a more gentle lover than her uncle, and smarter as well. He'd been to college. He was obsessed with movies. That's how they spent their time, at movie theaters or watching movies late into the night. Ivan never told her how he earned money, but she assumed he was on the payroll of one of the local gangsters. They went to parties at small mansions overlooking the Long Island Sound. She knew that as long as she continued living with Ivan it would be impossible for Irene to join her. She wrote her friend daily. They had imagined that they would be separate no longer than three months, but already a year had passed. Marina had underestimated the amount of money needed to find an apartment in New York. At least, with Ivan, it wasn't necessary for her to work. She went to school at night, taking art history classes and English, until her English was almost perfect and she could get a teaching job. Ivan didn't care whether she worked or not. He was often out of town, doing jobs for Boris, the gangster boss, which was fine with Marina, who preferred being alone so she could write letters to

Irene, whose parents were dying in Odessa. She told her friend everything: how she lost her virginity to her uncle in the basement and how Ivan stole her away. She told her about the ocean, the endless boardwalk past Coney Island where she walked every day. She told her about her classes at school, and later her job as a teacher. They talked in their letters about all the things they would do together, imagining the moment of their reunion. It was as if they had never left their bed in the room in Odessa where Irene's baby had died in the middle of the night.

Marina, who worked five days a week in a private school in Brooklyn Heights, was saving her money. She received a Masters in Fine Arts from Hunter College. She had always been a goal-oriented person. Her classmates in Odessa had always hated her for doing well in subjects like chemistry or Latin. The goal, in this case, was Irene, reuniting with her friend. But even if Marina had her own apartment, Irene couldn't leave her parents. Her father had Parkinson's and sat in a wheelchair most of the day with his head on his chest. Her mother had had a heart attack and walked with a cane. Irene knew if she went to the United States she would never see them again. She would feel guilty forever. Even though they had banished her from their house when she was pregnant with Sasha, she still felt obliged to accompany them through the final stages of their illnesses. And it was the final stages. Both of them spent more time in the hospital than at home and her father's legs were becoming gangrenous from spending too much time in bed. She sat at the edge of his bed and fed him bits of chocolate, but the melted chocolate, which he couldn't swallow, seeped out of the corners of his mouth. Irene wrote to Marina that after a day in the hospital she was tempted to go to the nearest bar and pick up some stranger and go home with him just to forget about everything, but that she managed to control herself and always ended up returning home alone, stopping first at the café where she and Marina used to drink their early afternoons cups of hot chocolate. Then she would walk along the desolate embankment looking out over the Black Sea, out into the middle of nowhere with the wind howling in her ears.

The only thing Ivan cared about was that Marina was in bed when he came home in the middle of the night. He would wake her up and force her to have sex, even though she had to be up at six in the morning in order to take the subway from Brighton Beach to Brooklyn Heights. Luckily, as a lover, he had simple tastes; for the few minutes that it lasted she could pretend that she was interested, and then fall asleep again while he lounged in bed next to her blowing smoke rings at the ceiling. Some nights he took movies of her lying naked on the bed. From behind the camera he would tell her to assume different positions. She would lie on the edge of the bed with her legs spread and masturbate, thinking of Irene, while Ivan roved around the room with his camera, pretending he was one of his heroes, Jean-Luc Godard or Frederico Fellini. Marina had no idea what he did with his movies, whether he sold them to his friends or spliced them into other cheaply made porno movies which were then distributed to video stores in Brooklyn. She wrote to Irene that Ivan preferred movies to sex, that he spent most of his time at home working on one of his many scripts, that he always went to bed long after she was already asleep.

One night, it must have been two in the morning, Marina received a phone call from a man whose voice she didn't recognize. "My name is Boris," the voice said, and Marina remembered meeting the man at one of the parties on Long Island. Ivan had introduced him to her as "my boss." Marina had heard other people talk about him as well. He was everyone's boss, it seemed. Later in the day, when the party at which she was introduced to him was almost over, she noticed him sitting in a lounge chair near the pool with his arms draped around the shoulders of two women in bikinis, girls really, young enough to be his children. "Is this Marina?" the man named Boris said over the phone, and at first she thought that he was going to order her to come and sleep with him, that he had depleted his supply of young women. Not only was he Ivan's boss, but he was the boss of Ivan's girlfriend as well. If she didn't sleep with him he would fire Ivan. Or perhaps, if she didn't do what he wanted, both of their bodies would be found floating facedown in the East River. She couldn't imagine any other reason why he was calling her at two in the morning.

"I have some news," he said. "Ivan is in jail. Don't ask me any questions. I want you to come to this address tomorrow"—he recited some numbers and she wrote them down—"and ask for a woman named Sheila. She'll give you all the details. Meanwhile"—he said this in Russian—"Ivan sends his love."

There were never any questions and there were never any answers. The woman named Sheila gave her an envelope containing ten thousand dollars. Ivan was in jail, she visited him in jail, he was sentenced to a year in jail in a prison in upstate New York. Every weekend she took the bus to visit him. Meanwhile, with the ten thousand dollars, she found a new apartment. That's what the woman named Sheila said: relocate, start a new life. Marina continued to teach art in the private school in Brooklyn Heights. Now she had enough money so she could talk on the phone frequently with Irene, at least once every other day. Both of Irene's parents had died and she was free to visit her friend in New York.

Almost five years had passed since the two women had seen one another and they spent most of their first weekend in bed, just like before. Irene could speak English as fluently as her friend. She had devoted five years to learning the language of her future. She had put her faith in Marina that coming to the United States would be her future. She had prepared herself for this moment. She stepped off the plane and there was her friend waving to her from behind a glass partition. They held hands in the back of the taxi that took them from the airport to the apartment. Irene said: "I know you've slept with many men. I forgive you. I slept with many men before I met you so now we're equal. But I've been faithful to you since you've been gone." Neither of them had ever slept with any other woman. They had learned the art of patience, of waiting. They drank vodka and ate spoonfuls of caviar sitting up in bed. They walked through the apartment naked. They admired themselves in the mirror. They combed each other's hair.

Every morning Marina went to work, and when she returned home Irene was sitting at the kitchen table reading a book in English.

"I'm going to read all the books on your shelf," she said.

Marina said: "He's going to be back soon. In a month he'll be out of jail."

She was referring to Ivan, of course. She had skipped her last visit to the prison to spend the weekend with Irene. She had made up an excuse about being sick, not knowing or caring whether Ivan believed her. The question was what to do when Ivan got out of jail. He knew that she had a new apartment and assumed that they would live together when he was released. The two women had enough money to escape, to disappear. Irene was interested in moving to California, a place neither of them had ever been. They could change their names. They could cut their hair. They could become different people. Irene stood at the ironing board in her bra and panties while Marina sat at the kitchen table drinking coffee. That was what they were doing on that August morning when Eddie Perez came in the window.

SECRET

I tell people my secrets in the hope that they'll tell me theirs. People think I'm an attentive listener but the only reason I talk to them is to use what they say in my writing. I ask them about the first time they fell in love or went to bed with someone. I ask them about their diseases. Their addictions. I get them to tell me things they never told anyone else. "I once hired a hit-man to kill my mother," she says, "but it all fell through at the last minute." "I slept with my shrink," she says. "I never told anyone this before." Maybe you'll recognize yourself in some of my stories, maybe not. Maybe everybody's stories are the same. Teeth. Everyone has problems with their teeth, but these aren't the stories I'm interested in. Root canals. Periodontal work. "I had an affair with my dentist," she says. "I never told anyone this before." She was the last patient of the day and he locked the door of his office behind him. There was a couch in a room behind his office, away from the bright lights and the X-ray machines and the plastic gloves. She had the feeling that she wasn't the first patient he had seduced. "I leaned over the arm of the couch and he lifted my skirt," she said. Sometimes people tell you more than you want to know. I had simply asked if she could recommend a dentist and this is what she told me. The affair with her dentist lasted three years. After he finished work on her teeth, they began meeting twice a week at a hotel near his office. They met during his lunch hour and eventually he left his wife and children. "But we never lived together," she said. I wanted to ask why but I had already heard too much. I was taking tylenol with codeine for the pain in my tooth and I was conscious of our thighs touching as we sat side by side in the booth in the back of the bar. It was closing time. I could imagine walking her home, climbing the stairs to her apartment, and making love to her without taking off my clothes. But then I remembered my wife, waiting at home, waiting up for me in our bed reading a book, and I didn't want to walk through the door with a secret of my own.

She was reading one of the long later novels by Henry James, *The Wings of the Dove,* I think. She was on page 320. My wife likes to talk about the books she's reading and I was familiar with *The Wings of the Dove,* I'd read it in college but I had forgotten the story, so hearing my wife talking about it was like rereading it. And I know I'll never have time to reread it. What I read, as I get older, what I tend to enjoy reading are biographies, life stories of people who overcame adversity, who performed heroic deeds under the worst circumstances, exile and imprisonment. I recently read a biography of Chairman Mao which had mostly to do with his sex life. Apparently, at all state functions, there was a room where Mao could go for a "rest," accompanied by two or three of his favorite consorts. I also read a biography of Bertolt Brecht which claimed that Brecht didn't write any of his major plays. That he had a group of women, his lovers, who wrote the plays. Elizabeth Hauptman. Ruth Eisler. There were others as well. Brecht always had two or three girlfriends at the same time. It seems odd to me that we remember Brecht's name but we don't remember the names of his collaborators. That he didn't even give these women credit for their work. That he cheated them out of royalties. That he never wrote a good play after they grew bitter and stopped working for him. They were in love with him and that's what inspired them to do his work and let him sign his name to the work they had written. They thought he would love them more, but he jilted them all instead.

I get into bed beside my wife and rest my head on the pillow while she continues to read. My wife and I have been married for fifteen years and sometimes we read aloud to one other before going to sleep. The main secret of our marriage is that she had an affair with another woman which lasted five years, and that half that time we lived separately from one another. But we're well past the point where we talk about that anymore, though for a long time, even after the affair ended, it was our main topic of conversation. "How's your tooth?" my wife asks. "It hurts," I say. "I'm going to the dentist tomorrow." And then she says: "Let me read this to you." I close my eyes and listen to the voice that begins and ends every one of my days, surrendering to the convoluted hum of sentences with no boundaries until my own thoughts are a blur of clouds and shadows on the distant horizon.

Memories, secrets, all my fantasies—everything fades under the hypnotic sway of my wife's voice—until all that remains is the dull pain in the side of my mouth.

A PLACE IN THE SUN

1

He started taking barbiturates after he finished filming *A Place in the Sun*. He began to fall down unexpectedly, and his friends didn't know what was wrong. They used to carry him home and when he got there he would crawl up the stairs to his room on his hands and knees. He would visit his old friend Libby Holman at her estate in Connecticut and they would take drugs together. Libby Holman's first husband had committed suicide and her son had died in a mountain accident. At the time, some of Monty's closest friends included Greta Garbo, Karl Malden, and Roddy Macdowell. Older friends, like Thornton Wilder, stopped coming around when they realized that Monty was addicted to pills. Monty was nominated for an Academy Award for his role as Clyde Griffiths in *A Place in the Sun* but he lost out to Humphrey Bogart for his portrayal of Charlie Allnut in *The African Queen*. Marlon Brando was also up for an Academy Award for his role as Terry in *On the Waterfront*. Monty's friends claimed that he didn't care whether he won the award or not. When they called him with the news he shrugged his shoulders. "I'm better than both of them," he said. Apparently Elizabeth Taylor had called him the night before the awards ceremony and told him she was sure that he was going to win. That Brando was a big phony. And that Bogart was too old.

2

It's possible he looked in the mirror and saw something he didn't want to see. His sexuality was a source of confusion, did he prefer men to women? Most of his fans were teenage girls who would be brokenhearted, to say the least, if they knew he liked to sleep with men. He always had a few women trailing after him as a kind of protection against the fear of anyone thinking he liked men more than women. The people who ran the movie studios would have fired him if they knew he preferred men. Some people say that this was one of the reasons he started drinking, but I don't think it's true. He could still function as an actor even though he was drinking heavily. He was already an alcoholic by the time he started preparing for the role of Prewitt in *From Here to Eternity*. Every woman who ever acted opposite him—Elizabeth Taylor, Jennifer Jones—fell in love with him. Jennifer Jones couldn't believe that he didn't want to sleep with her. It was possible for them to have sex without even speaking, as far as she was concerned. People get angry when they don't get what they want. When Monty rejected her, Jennifer stuffed a mink coat down the toilet, a present from her present husband, Vittorio de Sica, the director of the movie in which she and Monty were costarring. There was a vial of sleeping pills in her purse and she thought of swallowing all of them as a way of proving to Monty that she couldn't live without him. She rehearsed in her mind what she could possibly say to Monty to seduce him into sleeping with her, but when she finally said it: "If you don't make love to me, I'll die," he laughed in her face.

3

He liked to buy books but rarely had time to read them. He went to Brentanos on 5th Avenue with Thornton Wilder and bought books by Kierkegaard and Camus. He began taking classes at the Studio School with Lee Strasburg and boxing lessons at Stillman's gym. It was 1947, two years before he began work on *A Place in the Sun*. "The more an actor knows about himself," Strasburg said, "the more he will be able to make use of himself." Monty resisted some of Strasburg's better-known techniques, especially the exercise called "Private Moments." Monty, when he performed the exercise in front of a class at the Studio School, would strip naked and ramble on about his mother, how his mother wanted to control his life. But it was hard for him to let go, especially in a room full of strangers. The point of the exercise was to break down inhibitions. The more you could express yourself, the easier it would be to get under the skin of someone else's character. Monty felt that the problem with method acting was that most of the actors ended up playing themselves and what he wanted to do was disappear inside the body of some other person. He was too much himself as it was, and acting was a way of escaping. Motivation was everything. This person whose role I'm playing is not myself. He used to go out for coffee with Marlon Brando after class. Both of them were born in Omaha, Nebraska, but other than that they had little in common. Brando liked to brag about all the people he'd slept with, while Monty never discussed his personal life with anyone. He'd disappear for a few days at a time and no one would know where he was. He returned to New York from Los Angeles in between movies so he could carry on his romantic life in private. As far as the public was concerned, he was dating a young actress named Terry Moore. There's a photo of them staring into each other's eyes which gives the impression that they just spent a week in bed together. But in fact they never even touched. The Barbizon Models of New York voted him the most eligible bachelor of 1948, the same year he was arrested on 42nd Street trying to pick up young boys. When he was first told that he was going to play opposite Elizabeth Taylor in *A Place in the Sun*, he said "Who the fuck is she?" He had read the novel by Dreiser, *An American Tragedy*, on which the movie was based, and was excited about playing the part of Clyde Griffiths.

At the same time, he was offered the script of *Sunset Boulevard,* which Billy Wilder told him he had written "just for you." He was also offered leading roles in *The Naked and the Dead* (screenplay by Lillian Hellman), *High Noon,* and *Look Homeward, Angel.* He always came back from Hollywood complaining that he wasn't treated like "a person" or "an actor" but "a hot property," the heir to Tyrone Power and Rudolph Valentino. But he was too sensitive to do what was necessary to become a star. Not ruthless enough.

4

By the time he started shooting *A Place in the Sun,* Monty was getting drunk every night. Yet he was still able to wake up early and get to work. He would stand in a cold shower for ten minutes and drink a glass of orange juice with vodka. Often he was required to wake up before dawn. No matter how much he'd had to drink the night before, he was never late. In a way, drinking was his way of relaxing when he finished working on a movie, but as usual he went too far. This was what impressed Elizabeth, who also liked to take everything to the limit, but often didn't have the nerve.

They were living in a hotel in Lake Tahoe, filming *A Place in the Sun.* Elizabeth shared a room with her mother but Monty often coerced her to sneak out late at night. They would sit on the wooden steps of the hotel and stare at the moon. He would pass her the bottle of Jim Beam and she would take a quick sip, wiping her mouth with the back of her hand. During the day her mother never left her side and at night she had to wait until her mother was asleep before she could sneak out of her room to meet Monty. "My mother would kill me," she said, "if she knew I was meeting you." Both Elizabeth and Monty were sick of their mothers, that's one thing they had in common, but Monty didn't want to talk about personal matters while he was working on a movie. He wanted to discuss *A Place in the Sun*. She couldn't believe that anyone could take acting so seriously. She wanted to become a better actress so she could impress him, so he would fall in love with her like most of the other men she had met in her short life. She couldn't understand why he wasn't attracted to her, didn't attempt to touch her, or kiss her, or even take her hand, that he was content just to sit on the steps of the hotel smoking cigarettes and talking about acting. It was cold in Lake Tahoe, there was snow in the air, and she wore a jacket over her nightgown. They talked about George Eastman and Angela Vickers, the names of the characters in the movie, based on the characters Clyde Griffiths and Sondra Finchley in the novel *An American Tragedy* by Theodore Dreiser. Sometimes, when her mother was asleep, she would sneak out and go to his room. She would knock on his door and when no one answered she would open it and looked inside and stare at the empty bed and the pages of the script scattered over the floor. When she asked him, the next morning, where he had been the night before, he shrugged mysteriously and said "out," making it clear that it was none of her business. It never occurred to her that he might be interested in men. "You have the greatest tits," he would say. They both had overbearing mothers. Elizabeth had bushy eyebrows; her arms were covered with hair. People around them, the other people working on the movie, assumed they were sleeping together. Someone started a rumor: He had seen them making out in a parked car. Or she had seen them emerging, hand in hand, from the forest late at night. Some people, like the gossip columnist Hedda Hopper, assumed that they were going to get married.

It was after he finished work on *A Place in the Sun* that he began taking pills: tranquilizers, vitamins, antidepressants, diuretics, barbiturates. He would swallow a handful of pills with a glass of wine over dinner. He kept the pills in the pockets of his jacket. He would empty the bottles of pills which his various doctors prescribed for him into his jacket pockets before he went out. He would order expensive dinners at restaurants and not eat anything. When he did eat, he lifted the food with his hands, ripping apart pieces of raw meat. Then he would stuff hunks of food into his mouth. He would drink and eat and swallow pills almost simultaneously as the people around him pretended not to notice. People were frightened of admonishing him for taking too many pills, for drinking too much. They were frightened he might become angry and they didn't want to risk losing his friendship.

5

Elizabeth Taylor met Nicky Hilton during the filming of *A Place in the Sun*. He was twenty-three. She was eighteen. Elizabeth's mother was overjoyed. Conrad Hilton, Nicky's father, was worth $125 million, a lot of money in 1949. He himself had been married to Zsa Zsa Gabor and was presently going out with singer-actress Ann Miller when his son introduced him to Elizabeth and her mother. Some people think that Conrad tried to seduce his future daughter-in-law, but Elizabeth denies that this ever happened. One of the reasons she was attracted to Nicky was because he encouraged her to continue her career, unlike her former boyfriends (former Notre Dame football star Glen Foley and a businessman from Florida), who had insisted that she quit her career and become a housewife. At least that's what Nicky told her when they first started sleeping together. Everyone ignored rumors that he had other girlfriends, that he liked to stay out all night drinking and gambling. All that mattered to Elizabeth's mother were the millions of dollars he would someday inherit. Nicky kept a crucifix next to his bed along with a gun and a stack of porno magazines. The reality of being married to someone as famous as Elizabeth Taylor began to surface on their honeymoon. Wherever they went there were crowds who wanted an autograph or a photograph and Nicky was lost in the shadows. He began staying out all night gambling. When Elizabeth wanted to sleep with him he pushed her away. "I'm sick of looking at your face," he told her. She was frightened of confiding in her mother; she knew about her mother's expectations and dreaded the moment when she would have to tell her that her marriage wasn't working. Fuck the money. Nicky hated being known as "Mr. Elizabeth Taylor." She had thought he was proud of her for being a famous actress, but in the end all he wanted was a traditional housewife. While filming *Father's Little Dividend,* the sequel to *Father of the Bride,* which she started working on when she returned from her honeymoon, she discovered she was pregnant. One day she fainted on the set, but by the time she got home she had already miscarried. This angered Nicky even more; he thought it meant that she would never have another baby, never be able to. While she was recovering from the miscarriage, he went deep sea fishing with his friends. Although her mother advised her to give him one more chance, Elizabeth filed for a divorce a month after she lost the baby.

6

A Place in the Sun opened in August 1951 at the Capitol Theater in New York. The National Board of Review of Motion Pictures named it the best picture of the year, but it lost the Academy Award to *An American in Paris*. The film critic Andrew Sarris wrote that Cliff and Taylor were "the most beautiful couple in the history of cinema." In the fall of '51, Elizabeth moved back to New York and she and Monty began to see each other every day. Elizabeth had become engaged to the English actor Michael Wilding. Again, as she had done before her marriage to Nicky Hilton, Liz said she would call off her marriage to Wilding if Monty was willing to marry her. At the time, Monty was living in a duplex apartment at 207 E. 61st Street with a young actor, giving him money, helping him with his career. All of Monty's other friends insisted that the actor was just using him. When he couldn't sleep, Monty would climb to the roof of his building and stare into the windows of other people's apartments. He would stare at people as they undressed or had sex. He would walk around Times Square, make eye contact with a guy in a doorway, and take him home. On weekends he visited Libby Holman on her estate in Stanford, Connecticut. His medicine cabinet was filled with antispasmodics, muscle relaxants, antidepressants, anticonvulsants, painkillers, paregorics, and decongestants. For two years after he finished work on *A Place in the Sun* he didn't make another movie.

Then, almost overnight, he signed contracts to star in *I Confess* (directed by Alfred Hitchcock), *Terminal Station* (directed by Vittorio de Sica), and James Jones's *From Here to Eternity*. There were long periods of lucidity when he felt perfectly normal. He could act normal, even if he wasn't. From looking at him, you couldn't tell that he had just swallowed a handful of antidepressants. Part of his charm was to get you to tell him your life story, but if you asked him a question about his personal life, he changed the subject. He made it clear that he wasn't going to answer any personal questions. When he said good night to his friends—that's when his real life began.

7

It was his habit, while working on a movie, not to drink during the day. He was studying for the role of Prewitt in *From Here to Eternity*. He must have read the book about ten times, making notes in the margin about the motivation of the character. He began taking trumpet lessons. He would spend days trying to figure out the phrasing of a single sentence. During the filming, he spent his nights drinking with James Jones and Frank Sinatra. Sinatra had just broken up with Ava Gardner (she had left him for someone else) and was threatening suicide, but Monty talked him out of it. He was good at giving advice to his friends about their problems, but he had no way of solving his own, and no one could help him. When he wasn't drunk, Monty would coach Sinatra on his role of Maggio in *From Here to Eternity*. "Monty had a special kind of pain," Jones once said. "A pain he couldn't share."

"He wanted to love women," Deborah Kerr said. She was his costar in *From Here to Eternity*, the woman on the beach with Burt Lancaster. The woman who rolls around on the sand in a bathing suit with Burt Lancaster. It's the famous scene where they run out of the water and begin making love on the sand. "He wanted to love women," she said, "but he was attracted to men." In those days he would collapse at parties from too much drinking and too many pills. When he finished filming *From Here to Eternity*, he went to Cape Cod and stayed with Mary McCarthy in Wellfleet. She diagnosed his behavior as "hebephrenic schizophrenia." One night he broiled a steak in the fireplace and then carved it into small pieces on the shag rug and served it to the guests. Monty was again nominated for an Academy Award for his role as Prewitt in *From Here to Eternity* but lost to William Holden. At the time, the new young star in Hollywood was James Dean, who claimed that Monty was his idol. Dean would call him constantly when they were both in New York just to hear the sound of Monty's voice on the phone.

When he was in Hollywood he stayed with Elizabeth, who was pregnant with her second child. He usually stayed with her when her husband, Michael Wilding, was off making a movie. They would stay up all night and she would complain to him about her relationship with her husband. When he had too much to drink he would lean over and kiss her on the side of the neck and tell her how beautiful she looked. It was just like the old days, when they worked together on *A Place in the Sun*. She would ask him if she had changed a lot since they first met. She would let him touch her breasts, like he used to do. They would sit on the couch and he would rest his head on her lap and they would stay up all night talking. Sometimes he would fall asleep with his head buried between her breasts and she wouldn't move for fear of waking him. She would stay up all night watching him sleep, his face pressed against her breasts like a baby.

He would get drunk and end up in bed with someone, man or woman. He often passed out and whomever he was with had to undress him and put him to bed. When he was in New York, Elizabeth would call him from Hollywood every night. She and Michael Wilding were breaking up, and she needed Monty's advice. She was frightened that she was going to end up living alone with two children. He and Elizabeth and Michael Wilding had spent so much time together in the last few years that people assumed they were all sleeping together. She convinced Monty to come to California so he could talk to her husband and convince him they should separate, that no matter how much he loved her they could no longer live together.

On May 12, 1956, Elizabeth and Michael had a party at their house in the hills above Los Angeles. They invited Monty but he didn't want to go. Just the night before, Wilding had visited him to talk about Elizabeth, to tell him how much he was in love with her. How impossible it was for them to live together. They were telephoning Monty on alternate nights; first Elizabeth would call, then Wilding. For some reason they assumed he could help them. He had a hard time falling asleep, even on the best of days, but it was impossible to fall asleep after listening to the litany of a failed marriage. The last thing he wanted to do was go to the party at Elizabeth and Michael's, but both of them called and begged him to come, just for awhile, just to put in an appearance. Wilding had back trouble and spent most of the party lying on the couch. Elizabeth, distracted by her problems, the fear of living alone with two young children once her marriage ended, could barely pour the wine without spilling it on the rug. Monty sat in the corner and didn't speak to anyone.

The accident occurred on the road leading out of the canyon. Kevin McCarthy, Mary McCarthy's brother, was in a car directly in front of Monty's and Monty kept bumping him from behind. It was as if he'd fallen asleep at the wheel and had lost control of the car. Before leaving the party, Monty had gone to the bathroom and taken half a dozen pills, mostly tranquilizers. Suddenly, McCarthy said, the lights of the car behind him disappeared and he heard a crash. He stopped his car and ran back to find Monty's car twisted around a telephone pole with Monty crumpled beneath the dashboard. He drove back to Elizabeth's and ordered someone to call an ambulance, but Liz insisted that she go to the scene of the accident. She pried open the back door and cradled Monty's bloody head against her breasts, stuck her fingers in his mouth to pry out his two front teeth, which were lodged in his throat, then rode with him in the back of the ambulance to the hospital. The front of her dress was covered with blood. After Monty was wheeled into the operating room she collapsed in the hallway outside his door.

It took more than nine weeks for Monty to recover, nine weeks (most of it spent in traction) before he could imagine going back to work. When the accident occurred, he was filming *Raintree County* with Elizabeth, the first movie they had made together since *A Place in the Sun*. His nose was broken, jaw crushed, teeth had to be reconstructed. A cerebral concussion. Somehow one of his friends smuggled a bottle of whiskey into the hospital. He drank martinis through a straw. He was anxious to get out of bed and finish work on *Raintree County*. Half the movie had been shot before the accident. Monty tried to convince himself that he looked the same, but his nose was bent out of shape, his mouth was twisted. His upper lip had been torn apart by the accident. His eyes were filled with pain. Once he started work he had to give himself shots of codeine every few hours. They were filming in Natchez and Elizabeth's health began to deteriorate as well. She suffered from heat exhaustion (her corset was too tight) and hyperventilation. A doctor prescribed choral hydrate but Monty was the person she called for advice in the middle of the night. Mike Todd, her new lover, had proposed marriage: should she do it? It was a scene they had already repeated dozens of times in the past and Monty was tempted to slam down the phone when he heard her voice whining at the other end. "You're the only person who can make me happy," she would say.

8

It's hard to live in this world and not feel an insatiable craving for objects and money (for all the objects money can buy). The most expensive jewelry can be yours if you want it. The ability to acquire things makes people feel good about themselves. It's also hard to feel free of the need to be around other people, easy to become addicted to their need for you, to become dependent on their need. All the drugs one requires in order to sleep for even a few hours and then the pills one also requires to get out of bed and function during a day that might require you to recite lines which you supposedly memorized the night before. All the pills and alcohol one needs to get through the day. Richard Burton, Elizabeth's fifth husband (don't forget Nicky Hilton, Michael Wilding, Mike Todd and Eddie Fisher) woke at two in the afternoon and drank a vodka with orange juice for breakfast, and then continued drinking until he fell into bed next to the most beautiful woman in the world, or so some people thought, but who had recently (to everyone's horror) tipped the scales at 180, and whose triple chin made her the butt of a million Joan Rivers jokes on late night TV:

"I took Elizabeth Taylor to Sea World, but it was so embarrassing. Shamu the Whale jumped up out of the water and Liz asked if he came with vegetables."

"I won't say she's fat, but she had a face-lift, and there was enough skin left over to make another person."

"She has more chins than the Chinese phonebook and loves to eat so much she stands in front of the microwave and yells 'Hurry.'"

One reason why people get divorced is because one or both members of the couple loses interest in sex. This is true of everyone. Desire fades with familiarity. You have to renew your feeling of desire or sublimate it so that you can accomplish other things. One way of renewing desire is to appeal to the other person's fantasies. Many people are too shy to confess what they would like to do in bed for fear that the person they're with would reject them or think they were crazy. You never know how another person is going to react to what you want to do in bed. For many people, what happens inside their fantasy world is more interesting than real life. Going to bed with someone whom you fantasize about is often a big disappointment.

The need for freedom is often stronger than the need for security (in this sense freedom means freedom to sleep with whoever you want), and it seems to be a fact of life that you can't have both. As a reaction to her marriage to Nicky Hilton, who beat her up in the shower and refused to sleep with her, even on their wedding night, she married a man twice her age, pipe-smoking Michael Wilding, an alcoholic as well (she didn't have a husband who wasn't addicted to alcohol or pills), and it was just a matter of time—in this case, a few years and two children later—before Wilding came home and found Liz ("don't call me Liz") in bed with Victor Mature. It's amazing that each of Elizabeth's husbands didn't assume that at some point she'd be unfaithful to them, or get tired of them, or find someone who (at least in the moment) seemed more interesting, or that the need to fall in love again (to experience the exuberance that accompanies meeting someone you love) would eventually become a more insistent need than creating or maintaining a relationship long past the initial excitement was over. Why bother? Eddie Fisher could make love twelve times a night but Elizabeth still wasn't satisfied. Richard Burton bought her the most expensive diamond in the world. It cost him $1.1 million, but she still wasn't happy.

9

She kept meeting men, falling in love, and getting married. Most of her marriages (Nicky Hilton, Michael Wilding, Mike Todd, etc.) overlapped: she began sleeping with her new husband while she was still married to her old one. She went off to make *Cleopatra* and Eddie Fisher came along as companion/nurse but that didn't stop her from starting a new relationship with Burton. Everyone was aware that Burton and Taylor were attracted to one another, including Fisher, but there was nothing anyone could do to stop them. Burton himself was married to Sybil Williams, but his wife accepted the fact that he often went off and seduced young actresses. Possibly "accept" isn't the right word. While Burton was away she would have an affair or two of her own, or so people say, and when she and Burton eventually split up she married a young musician named Jordan Christopher. The idea of a woman making love to a man twenty years younger was shocking to a lot of people, who assumed that something was wrong with the man for preferring an older woman when he could be with someone his own age or younger.

It was just a matter of time before the gossip columnists, Hedda Hopper and Louella Parsons, found out that Richard Burton and Elizabeth Taylor were having an affair. They were seen huddled together in conversation at a party and that was enough to get people talking. Someone saw them standing alone on a balcony. Someone saw them kissing in the backseat of a taxi. There was a rumor that at a birthday party for Rex Harrison, who played the role of Julius Caesar in *Cleopatra,* they went into the bathroom together and didn't come out for twenty minutes. Someone said they saw them get into the backseat of Burton's limousine and drive into the country and park at the end of a deserted road. Someone thought they saw them leaving a hotel in the south of France. It was possible to say anything about anyone and then read about it in the gossip columns the next day as if it were true. Elizabeth and Eddie would go to parties together and she would go off with Richard and Eddie would try to find her and force her to leave but she would laugh in his face. She would humiliate him publicly. Once Eddie caught them fucking in a back bedroom at a party and moved into a hotel for a few days but Elizabeth found out where he was staying and ordered him to come back. She denied the fact that she and Burton were involved even though Fisher had seen them together with his own eyes. "We were just drunk,"

Elizabeth said, as if that excused everything. They were always drunk, so what did it matter, and of course Eddie returned; if Liz asked him to do something he did it, even though everyone referred to him (as people had done with Nicky Hilton and Michael Wilding) as "Mr. Elizabeth Taylor." Possibly the attraction of being married to Elizabeth was the idea that you were doing something every other man in the world fantasized about doing, and maybe all the husbands knew that the marriages weren't meant to last but decided that a few years or a few nights with Elizabeth was worth it. No one cared about getting Nicky Hilton's autograph; he might as well have been Elizabeth's chauffeur for all anyone cared. It was hard not to pale in comparison when you were around Elizabeth; the only husbands with any real stature were Mike Todd and Richard Burton. And there was also the fact that she was "great in bed," or so Eddie Fisher reported, "totally pornographic." He said she used to crawl around on the floor and he would fuck her from behind. Eddie Fisher, who received amphetamine injections three times a week, was capable of making love twelve times a night. Five minutes after having an orgasm he was ready to fuck again. He had left his wife, Debbie Reynolds, to marry Elizabeth. Everyone thought that he and Reynolds had an idyllic marriage, but in fact they fought constantly and rarely slept together. Elizabeth was blamed for breaking up a marriage that was about to end or shouldn't have existed. Elizabeth didn't mind if he slapped her around—she seemed to like it—while Debbie wouldn't even let him go down on her. What a bore. Eddie had been the best friend of her third husband, Mike Todd, who was killed in a plane crash flying from Burbank, California to New York on the night of March 21, 1958 in an airplane called *Liz*. After Todd was killed, Eddie visited Liz every day. She was Todd's widow and he was Todd's best friend so it made sense for them to try to console one another. At least that was the role he decided to play. No one's quite sure how long it took before they started sleeping together. Todd was like Hilton: he thought that women wanted to be abused. He would insult Elizabeth publicly, put his hands down the front of her dress in the middle of a formal dinner party, cup her enormous breasts in his palms in front of a hundred guests. He would refer to her as "my cunt" and complained to anyone who would listen when she started gaining weight. They liked to fight publicly as a prelude to going to bed together. Elizabeth would turn on anyone who tried to stop them and tell them to mind their fucking business. Sex was better if it was preceded by a fight. Todd didn't hit her, like Hilton had done; he preferred humiliation, forcing her to beg for sex if she wanted it, and then denying her anyway. Todd hid a tape recorder under their bed, turned it on when they were fucking, and gave copies of the tapes to his friends. With Fisher, she was in charge; it was her turn to humiliate him. She alternated between violent types (Hilton, Todd) and passive types (Wilding, Fisher), but that all changed when Burton entered her life.

10

After the car accident, the studio suspended production of *Raintree County* for nine weeks—long enough, they hoped, for Monty to recuperate. In fact, the injuries he suffered during the accident never totally healed. During this time Elizabeth and Michael Wilding broke up. There was a rumor that she was having an affair with Frank Sinatra, that she had become pregnant again and Frank was the father. Libby Holman, who blamed Elizabeth for Monty's accident, called her "a heifer in heat."

She was having an affair with a cameraman named Kevin McClarny and they were contemplating getting married when McClarny introduced her to his boss, Mike Todd, who at the time was seeing Evelyn Keys, the actress who had played Scarlet O'Hara's younger sister in *Gone With the Wind*. Keys, before she met Todd, had been married to both King Vidor and John Huston. Mike Todd had been married a few times as well, first to Bertha Fisher, who stabbed herself accidentally when she was chasing her husband around the house with a steak knife, and a second time to the actress Joan Blondel. When Todd and Taylor met they dumped all their current lovers.

In order to alleviate the pain from the accident, Clift was taking more pills and drinking more than he had done before, if that's possible. One night he was arrested for "indecent exposure." He had taken off his clothes and walked down the main street of Danville, Kentucky, where the film was being made. When he was arrested, the police found 250 vials of assorted pills in his hotel room.

Todd called Elizabeth every day when she was filming *Raintree County*. He sent her a bouquet of 200 long-stemmed roses. He sent her a $30,000 black pearl ring. He flew her to Chicago in his private plane. Of all her friends, only Monty tried to discourage her from getting married yet again. He advised her against marrying someone so much older than she was (as Wilding had been), but after her marriage to Nicky Hilton she was wary of younger, volatile types, though in a way Todd was more like Hilton than Wilding, a stay-at-home pipe-smoking Englishman (at least on the surface) who, according to his friend Stewart Granger, had his "balls busted" by Elizabeth. Elizabeth and Monty didn't see much of each other during her marriage to Todd.

On a yacht near Miami, Elizabeth injured her back and ruptured two spinal discs. Surgery was only partially successful and she had to spend two weeks convalescing.

Todd's idea of women was that they liked to be mistreated. He used to drag Elizabeth around by the hair. With Wilding she had played the role of dominatrix, but with Todd she would be submissive. She preferred taking orders to giving them. Her marriage to Todd was her third in five years.

"I don't care what people think about me as long as I have my children, my new husband, and my friends." Taylor said. "I can't worry about fifty million other people. What do I owe my public? Do I owe my life to them? No, I owe exactly what they see on the screen, and if they don't like it, they don't have to pay to watch me act."

11

Even the people closest to Monty Clift were unable to understand why he acted the way he did, and after awhile he stopped trying to analyze himself. The socalled psychiatrist who was supposed to help him ended up prescribing pills and medicines that only made his problems worse. Who was the person who invited people to his townhouse on the Upper East Side of Manhattan and then passed out while all the people around him pretended that nothing was wrong? These people literally stepped over his body as if falling asleep on the living room floor was a normal thing to do.

By the time she began filming *Cleopatra* in 1960, Elizabeth Taylor was suffering from headaches, toothaches, eye strain, back spasms, and coughing spells. She was also accident prone, breaking her leg or pulling a muscle in her leg, and when she was filming *Elephant*

Walk a shard of glass flew in her eye and she was in the hospital for a week. There was never a time when she wasn't taking pills, painkillers and sleeping pills, drinking nonstop, and demanding everyone around her to do whatever she wanted, including her husband—in 1960, it was Eddie Fisher—who had to accept, as well, that she might be sleeping with someone else, which was invariably a fact of their life. One could only imagine what might happen if he was ever unfaithful to her. "I never dreamed about sleeping with anyone else," Eddie said. "Being Elizabeth Taylor's lover is a full time job."

12

Theodore Dreiser pressed his face against the window of the restaurant. It didn't matter what was behind the glass; all he knew was that he wanted it, wanted a taste, at least, wanted to see what it felt like, "it" being anything he didn't have. He was poor. He had been born poor. There was the window and he was on the other side of it looking in and there was the fear that he might always be there, that he was doomed to always be on the outside looking in. He had read Herbert Spencer; he knew that only the fit survive, that the unfit were culled out for the betterment of the race, that a bad fate meant you had a bad character, that desires ("nascent excitations") were what made people act and that people acted to avoid feeling pain. It occurred to Dreiser that he was the type of person who secretly desired to feel unhappy, who sabotaged relationships, who hated himself, who would grow old sitting on a park bench munching a day-old sandwich he had found in the trash, that he was as ugly as he thought he was and no one would love him and if someone did love him he would push them away. Now there was another window and behind the glass people were eating colorful mounds of steaming food from plates glazed with blue flowers and drinking champagne from thin-stemmed glasses. Couples mainly: the man lifts his glass and proposes a toast ("Here's to us") while the woman (twenty years younger, at least) tosses her hair out of her eyes and raises her bare shoulders like a swan, a statue of a swan, as inert and dumb as any statue might be, but beautiful nonetheless, and willing to do anything to please the man sitting opposite her. The woman reminded Dreiser of his sister Emma, on whom he later modeled the character of Carrie in his novel *Sister Carrie* and who had fled the poverty of family life in Chicago by running off with a married man to New York. The man had been relatively successful in Chicago but in New York he was a failure. It was strange to Dreiser that women had the power to use their beauty to escape their lives, but he didn't have anything. He would return to his flophouse and lie awake thinking of the woman in the restaurant and what it would feel like to bury his face between her legs. He thought of his fiancée, Sara, who was in Missouri with her family, and then he would think of the woman in the restaurant, then back to Sara, who refused to sleep with him until they were married. His fantasies about having sex with the woman in the restaurant would keep him awake most of the night and he would doze off at dawn wondering if marrying Sara was the appropriate thing for him to do. He imagined that once he married Sara he would be happy lying next to her in bed every night and that he would never even dream of making love to anyone else, that it was possible to be content making love to one person for his entire life. He wasn't certain what he felt for Sara (whom he, and everyone else, called "Jug"), but it was easy to convince himself that he was in love with her from a distance. The last time he visited her in Missouri he tried to convince her to have sex, but she had pushed him away and he had refused to talk to her for an hour, sitting at the opposite end of the sofa chain-smoking while she wept. It was only when they were saying goodbye that she allowed him the liberty of touching her bare skin. He could feel her whole body turn rigid as he pressed his lips to the side of her neck. After he kissed her, she wiped her mouth with the back of her hand when she thought he wasn't looking. There was nothing for him to do in New York except pay women to sleep with him or jerk off in his tiny room thinking of the woman in the restaurant. Sara's image paled in comparison to this woman, and to the other women he passed on the street. On nights when he couldn't sleep he wandered the banks of the East River contemplating suicide; then he would return to his room and write a sixty page letter to Jug. During the day he forced his way into the offices of newspaper editors demanding a job, anything, and when he was turned down he came back the next day on his hands and knees and did it all again. There was no way he could ask Jug to come to New York to be with him if he didn't have a job, a livelihood, a career, a means of supporting both of them. What he had was perseverance, which is different from faith, and a talent for writing quickly without worrying about syntax, and an obvious sympathy for the people he saw on the streets. If there was a clause dangling at the end of a sentence some copy editor at the newspaper or magazine could lop it off, as far as Dreiser was concerned; there was always something to write about, something to capture his attention, and rewriting what he had already written was someone else's job. He could write about anything. He would interview politicians and writers and the heads of corporations like Andrew Carnegie and ask them how they had managed to escape their humble origins in the hope that he would learn what was necessary to become a success in the world. At one time, they had stood with their faces pressed to the window, on the outside looking in. He assumed that the readers of the magazines were like him, frustrated with the cards life had dealt, and like him they were fascinated with success stories, the intersection between talent and luck and ambition, how you could be poor one day and rich the next, and whether one could be true to one's ideals and still get ahead in the world, how it was possible to get ahead without stabbing anyone else in the back. But Dreiser's own success fantasy was always one step ahead of itself. What he wanted to know was what happened to you after you achieved success. "If you don't have anything," people say, "you have nothing to lose," but if you have something it can be taken away from you, could slip through your fingers like sand through a sieve. One day you would be having dinner in Delmonico's or Sardi's, the two fanciest restaurants of the time, your fork raised in midair above a plate as you told the woman opposite you how you spent your day—"You can't imagine how much money I make doing nothing"—and the next day you could be on the benches with the birds, feeding the birds the crumbs of someone else's half-eaten sandwich.

13

The water is cold and she has her period and her mother screams at the director, George Stevens, and says if he insists that Elizabeth dive into the water she'll sue the studio, if anything happens she'll hold him responsible, if running into the water while she has her period makes it impossible for her to have babies she'll do her best to blacklist him. But he just laughs at her and Monty chases Elizabeth around the lake and they lie on the grass at the water's edge, his head resting on her stomach while she plays with his hair, pretending to be in love with her.

Some nights, when neither of them can sleep, they sit on the wooden steps of the old hotel, smoking, looking out at the trees or up at the sky, naming the constellations, Monty pointing out things to her that she would never see on her own. Sometimes they rehearsed together, Monty sipping from a silver flask. Even on the coldest night he never wore anything warmer than a lightweight sport jacket, his shirt unbuttoned down to his waist, while Elizabeth huddled in a fur coat, wearing only a flimsy nightgown underneath. He passes her the flask and she tilts her head back and swallows, wanting to be as much like him as possible, her coat falling open so he can see her bare legs.

Most of the time they talk about their mothers. Monty's mother was obsessed with the idea that he was descended from royalty. She spent her whole life trying to discover his family lineage. She sent him to boarding school in Europe where he learned French and German. He speaks German perfectly, fluently, and Elizabeth is stunned that he knows so much more than she does, that it's possible to learn anything, that not only is Monty intelligent, he's intuitive as well and can often tell what Elizabeth is feeling before she speaks, can literally read her mind. The only thing Elizabeth knows is how to use her beauty to get what she wants, to lure men with the fantasy that she might sleep with them some day. The only other thing she knows is what it feels like to be in front of a camera, to "make love to the camera" as Marilyn Monroe said she tried to do. Ever since she was twelve and starred opposite Mickey Rooney in *National Velvet* that's what she's been doing. Signing autographs, auditioning for roles. Staring at herself in the mirror. Her mother tagging along behind her.

"She's such an asshole," she says to Monty, the only person on the planet who understands what she's feeling.

She longs for the time that she can be on her own, that she can stay out all night if she wants. She wonders if Monty's reluctance to sleep with her (if he puts his hands between my legs, I'll let him, I'll let him do anything) has to do with her mother. It never occurs to her that he isn't interested in sleeping with women.

14

We were on a boat going to Europe. Me, my mother, my twin sister Roberta, my brother Brooks. I was only nine years old but can remember it all as if it happened yesterday. I was playing in the outdoor pool on the upper deck of the ship when this boy—a few years older than I was—held my head under water. I tried to struggle—where was my mother, anyway?—but he was too strong. We were going to Europe, my father was back in New York. My mother couldn't stay in one place for more than a few months; she was constantly dragging us back and forth between the United States and Europe. William, my father, never came on these trips. He had lost a lot of money in the stock market crash and had to work like a mongrel dog to keep the family above water. There was a rumor that he had a girlfriend in New York, and who can blame him? I know that my mother didn't want him to come along when we went to Europe. We were playing—I was playing alone—in the shallow end of the pool when this guy whose name I didn't know but who I had seen around the pool every day since the trip began twisted my arm behind my back and pushed my head underwater. Whenever I tried to escape I felt his grip tighten. I was on my knees, tearing my skin on the bottom of the pool. Where was my mother? All anyone ever told me was that when I tried to get away a gland burst in the side of my neck and when we reached Germany I had to stay in the hospital for a month with a fucking cast around my head. I can still see the guy's face: bronze skin, high forehead, shifty blue eyes. I've always been attracted to people who don't look at you directly and I'll never know what motivated him. Something I did that made him want to inflict pain on me. That threatened him. People always ask me about the scar on the right side of my neck and I always tell them that it was my mother's fault. When I was younger, I never dreamed of disobeying my mother. But now I can't wait to tell everyone how she ruined my life.

15

Monty had an acting career on Broadway before he went to Hollywood. It never occurred to him that he would one day become a movie star. Just the term "movie star" seemed to reduce the art of acting to its lowest common denominator. Clark Gable, for instance. A household name, to say the least. A face that everyone recognized when he appeared in public. A man who could sleep with a different woman every night, if that was what he wanted. One of the advantages of being a movie star was that everyone wanted to sleep with you just to be able to say they had done it. There were no emotional strings attached.

The high point of his Broadway career was his performance in a play called *There Shall Be No Night* by Robert Sherwood. The play starred Alfred Lunt and Lynn Fontaine, two of the most famous stage actors of their time. Monty had just returned from Mexico, where he had spent most of his time in his hotel room suffering from dysentery. He had spent a week in a clinic in New Orleans, taking drugs to ease the pain, but he had suffered irreparable damage to his intestines, from which he never fully recovered.

There Shall Be No Night opened in 1940. What Monty learned from working with Alfred Lunt was never to waste a gesture, to make every tone of voice mean something. He imitated the older actor, who played the part of his father. It was during the run of *There Shall Be No Night* that Monty began to distance himself from his mother. He rented a house in upstate New York, in a town where other actors and playwrights owned houses, and began to go up there every weekend. His mother insisted on visiting him; just the thought that she was coming and Monty would withdraw into himself, become sullen and angry. Ethel was oblivious to the way her son was reacting to her and there was nothing he could do or say to prevent her from interfering with his life.

Everyone wanted to sleep with Monty. He loved being around women but he rarely went to bed with them. "We settled for friendship," one of his earliest girlfriends confessed. Women would fall in love with him, as Elizabeth did on the set of *A Place in the Sun*, refusing to believe that he wasn't interested in sleeping with women. Most of the women he met were ignorant of the possibility of men loving men or women loving women. Most of the actors and actresses whom Monty met were in love with themselves.

16

Elizabeth practically fainted when she heard that she was going to play opposite Montgomery Clift in a movie based on.... but she had never heard of the novel *An American Tragedy,* much less the author. "It's a great book," her agent said. "You should read it." She had never made a movie based on a book before and the only reading she did were the scripts that were offered to her. Reading wasn't high on her agenda. She had performed miserably at the school which was created in the MGM studio for child actors like herself, teenagers like Roddy McDowell and Shirley Temple. She had performed adequately at first, but soon became bored. The only thing she was interested in studying was her image in the mirror. She couldn't see the purpose of spending a few precious hours of each day trying to decipher mathematical equations or memorize words of a foreign language, though she was always impressed when an adult inserted a word of French into a sentence and for a moment she wanted to be like that person too, educated, refined, intelligent, self-assured. But as long as she was beautiful she didn't have to worry about what she knew or didn't know. Men would compliment her on her intelligence as a way of getting her into bed and she would laugh in their faces because she knew she was really stupid. Knowledge takes on different forms. As long as people told her she was beautiful she would have nothing to worry about, and people never stopped telling her that she was the most beautiful woman on the planet. The only person who ever criticized her was her mother. And Monty. He would tease her about the thick patches of hair covering her arms. He would tell her that her legs were too heavy, which was true. "You have great tits," he would tell her. No one had ever spoken to her like that. She would always refer to her breasts as "my tits." All the clothing she wore was chosen to alert the world to the size of her breasts, and she took delight in leaning forward so that the man or woman whom she was talking to could stare down the front of her dress. She would watch the person's eyes as they flickered from her face to her tits and then up again and then back. Did he really think I didn't know he saw them? There were some guys who stared at her tits and didn't even bother looking at her face. What interested her most about Monty was that he didn't look at her at all. Neither her breasts or her face seemed to interest him particularly. What he wanted to do was talk about acting. She had never met anyone who was so serious about what he was doing. Most of the other people she worked with turned the idea of making a movie into a joke. The whole purpose of making a movie was to dupe as many people as possible into thinking that the people on the screen were real. The purpose of making movies was to make as much money as possible. This was true of everything in the country now that the war was over and people were too bored to do anything but think about making money. This was Clyde's problem in *An American Tragedy* as well. Dreiser's book, and then the movie, were mirrors of something that no one wanted to admit. All anyone cared about in Hollywood was to get your picture into the newspaper or appear on the cover of the fan magazines as often as possible. Did people turn their heads when you walked down the street? Did waitresses ask for your autograph?

When she first met Monty she was still a virgin. It was shortly after she began work on *A Place in the Sun* that she slept with Nicky Hilton. And that was that. From then on there was a lot of sex with as many different people as possible. Not with Nicky, who was drunk most of the time and preferred beating her up to having sex. Monty, of course, thought she was a fool for marrying him. He predicted that the marriage wouldn't last for more than a year and he was right.

"If only you had married me," Elizabeth said, weeping, on the telephone, New York to California, when she decided to end her first marriage. She wrote love letters to Monty, all during the filming of *A Place in the Sun*, and afterward, when she was married to Hilton, and Monty would read them aloud to all his latest boyfriends. They would laugh about it all, take more drugs, and laugh some more. The difference between Monty and Elizabeth was that he had read *An American Tragedy*, just as later he would read *From Here to Eternity* before making the movie, that he could speak German fluently, as well as

French and Italian, that acting was a way of escape from this alien body, and that becoming the character in the movie or play was the only form of sanity he knew.

MYSTERIOSO

I'd been meeting Vincent Cardozo once a week at the Hotel Albert on University Place. The hotel was around the corner from the old Cedar Tavern where all the famous abstract expressionist painters, like Kline and Pollock and de Kooning, used to hang out in the 1950s. It had been renovated beyond recognition since that time (the original Cedar was actually a few blocks south), but it would never lose its old reputation, a landmark in the history of the New York art world. Vincent, in his way, was part of that world. He attended all the black-tie openings at the Metropolitan Museum and the Museum of Modern Art; occasionally, I'd see his photo in the society pages of the Sunday papers. It was too bad that we never had time to talk about the things we did when we were apart. Mostly we just had sex in room 19 on the 3rd floor and then he left. Smoked a Marlboro Light down to the filter while getting dressed. "I have to run," he would say, kissing me on both cheeks. "I'll see you next time."

I would lie in bed after he was gone, inhaling the smoke he'd left behind, his odor on the sheets. Once, when I was lying there, feeling anonymous and like I was about to fall asleep, the bars of an old show tune floated up from the air shaft and I sang along. The walls were lemon-colored and the paint was flaking off the ceiling. I could hear voices from other rooms. People bickering in shadowy languages I couldn't understand. Sighs of contentment. I felt like I was moving from the periphery of my life into the center, trading off illusions. A naked woman in a hotel room counting off the seconds until it was time to go.

During the days when we didn't see each other we would try to talk on the phone, but never for more than a few minutes at a time. "I'll see you on Friday," I would say, and he would repeat it back to me like a parrot. "Friday, I'll see you Friday." In six months neither of us had ever canceled. I'd become dependent, in my way, on the time we spent together, a respite from my life with Dean, who was out of town more often than not and seemed oblivious to my secret life.

Yet I wasn't surprised when I arrived at the Albert on a sweltering mid-June afternoon, having told my husband the usual excuse—"I'm going shopping with a friend"—and the old man behind the desk adjusted his bifocals and handed me a page torn from a memo pad with the words "I'll see you next week" written across the top, followed by the initial "V." Either Vincent had arrived in person with the note or had hired a messenger to deliver it, but I didn't stop to question the hotel clerk: what did it matter? What mattered was that I was secretly relieved at the interruption in our routine, that our affair had become a routine without either of us realizing it, and that canceling for the first time was the beginning of the end, at least in some unspoken way. Most of all I was happy it was Vincent who had made the first move.

I crumpled the note in my fist but didn't drop it in a wastebasket until I passed the Cooper Union library and continued east into the neighborhood which I called "home" when I first moved to New York. The reality of the hotel room had already receded into the past, the recent past, since I knew there would be other afternoons, more whispering beneath the sheets. More of the dream life was up ahead, whether with Vincent or someone else.

There was a cafe across the street from your apartment on St. Mark's Place, between First Avenue and Avenue A, where I'd sat before, on afternoons like this one when I had time to kill. This was my destination, whether I knew it or not. I sat at the table near the window reading *The Wings of the Dove,* but not really reading; instead, every minute or two, I looked up from the book and stared at the steps of the tenement leading to the door of your building.

Little did I know that in two weeks Vincent would be dead (how naïve we had been not to think that my husband had paid the man behind the desk at the hotel to spy on us) and that I'd be sharing your apartment. That Dean, who was responsible for Vincent's death, or so I assumed, if not as the actual murderer then as the person who hired someone to kill him, was searching for me, along with the police. That my photo would appear alongside Vincent's—"Wife of movie producer sought in murder of mayor's aide"—on the front pages of all the newspapers.

There you are, coming down the street, looking not much older than when I last saw you standing in front of the classroom. Does it shock you that I introduce myself? Just because I was one of your ex-students doesn't give me the license to invade your life. You say you remember me but I know it isn't true. You're just being polite, embarrassed, and I watch you try to hide your annoyance when you realize I know you're lying. You're a different person than you were then and there's no reason why you should remember me. You had published a novel, you're working on another book. That's what is on your mind, or so you told me later, when I run into the street and present myself to you as "your former student." All I can do is write my name and phone number on a scrap of paper you rip out of the spiral-bound pad you're carrying in your hand, not thinking that Dean will be suspicious if you call and ask for me, not telling you I'm married. No doubt Dean was already suspicious of Vincent; he had known, for months, that I was sleeping with someone else, but pretended he didn't.

"And you, what do you do? Are you still in school?"

I want to tell you about all the stories I've written, some of which have been published in magazines with names like *Lingo* and *Pequod*, which I know you've never seen. I want to tell you how much I like your book, even though saying this isn't the total truth. It was only when we were finally together, after we had made love at least a half-dozen times on the futon on the floor of your bedroom, that I felt free enough to tell you where I thought it had gone wrong. I would realize, then, that you didn't want me to tell you what a great book it was, that you needed feedback, real criticism, that you yourself had reservations about what you had done, that the last thing you wanted in a lover was a sycophant, someone who would lick your feet no matter what. You were having problems with your next book; the publishers apparently wanted you to write a sequel, using the same main character, the policeman who solved the murder of the dead prostitute and who fell in love with a Russian woman. "I'm not interested in this shit anymore," you said. "I'm going crazy." You wanted to write about Hitler. Not Hitler, specifically, but the Nazis. The neo-Nazis. The skinheads. Something, it wasn't clear. All you could do was read books and hope for some inspiration. All you could do was study the books others had written. You wanted to write something that no one else had ever written, and in a new form, but you doubted whether your publishers would be interested. You had spoiled them by producing the kind of commodity that many people seemed to enjoy. Your first book was already in its tenth printing (hard covered). The paperback rights had been sold for $300,000. Foreign rights as well. Germany, France, Japan.

All this you tell me as we stand on the sidewalk outside your building.

"I'm having coffee," I say, nodding toward the window of the cafe and the table where I'd left my bag.

And you say: "I'll call you tonight if you like."

How can I tell you that I've been anticipating this moment for five years? I want to ask you if you remembered the night in the coffeehouse after class when you touched my arm and suggested that I read the poems of Anna Akhmatova. How it was you, without knowing it, who encouraged me to be a writer.

I remember the silence in the classroom when the chairman of the department announced that you had been fired. The chairman himself was going to replace you for the rest of the semester. Of course, Margaret, the woman who accused you of raping her, had left the class long before. It was practically the only thing any of the students talked about. And not only us, your students, it was everyone on the campus. There were articles about it in *The Village Voice* as well. And of course, in those articles, we learned that you had been fired once before for the same reason. That you had slept with a student at your previous job. The same thing had happened. A reporter from *The Voice* even called me up and asked whether you had ever tried to seduce me. I hung up on him. We were all on your side by then. Possibly sleeping with students, we argued, was the best way to teach them anything. After every class, we debated the ethics of whether a teacher should go to bed with his or her students. We couldn't understand why anyone should care. We couldn't believe that Margaret's accusation—"He raped me"—was being taken seriously.

My father began talking to me in German when I was five. He'd say simple things like "Wie geht es?" (How are you?) and ask me to repeat the words back to him. "Guten nacht," he would say when he kissed me good night. He had been teaching German literature in translation at Columbia when he was offered a similar job at Sarah Lawrence. I don't know why he chose one job over another. Maybe he felt it was time for a change. Maybe he didn't want me to grow up in New York City.

I was seven at the time. My parents didn't consult me about moving. My mother, I know, wasn't particularly happy about making the move. One day we were living in a rambling apartment in one of the prewar buildings on West End Avenue. Next minute we're in a house, our own house, with a staircase and a basement. There was a hallway with rooms (our bedrooms) and a study for my father with a ceiling-to-floor bookcase. Apparently another professor and his family had lived there before us but he had died and they had moved away. The house smelled like something had been cooking on the stove for too long. Like the kitchen walls had been lacquered with grease. The professor who had lived there, Dr. Horowitz, had actually died in the house, in the bedroom where my parents now slept, so maybe the smell in the air was the residue of his long illness, the smell of bedpans and mentholatum that accompanies any disease. I always wanted to ask my parents when and why Dr. Horowitz had died—how long before we moved in—but I never did. Maybe it was just the smell of dead leaves. The house was surrounded by evergreen and elm trees and when we moved in the leaves were changing color. In a few months they began petrifying on their branches and then falling to the ground like dead birds. It was my job, with my father, to rake the leaves into black garbage bags and prop them against a tree where the local garbage men would pick them up. Now that the leaves were gone I could see the street from my bedroom window, and all the other houses up and down our block, through the empty branches. I could smell the burning leaves in the air.

One of the best things about living out of the city was that I could walk to school by myself, though at first my mother took me, hand in hand, down the cool suburban tree-lined streets. It's easy, she said. One block, two blocks, and then you're there. I saw other children, some with parents, others on bicycles, all heading in the same direction, all converging on our little prison. It was just a matter of time before I would get to know these children. I would memorize their names and addresses. My mother would drop me off at their homes on Saturday afternoons and we would sit around a gaping fireplace playing party games like pin-the-tail-on-the-donkey or rainy afternoon board games like Monopoly and Clue. My least favorite game involved apples bobbing in a vat of cold water. I remember trying to get the apple but it would always fall back in, and feeling dizzy and sick, at one party, after spinning around with a blindfold, so sick that the mother of the child who was giving the party got worried and called my mother, who interrupted whatever she was doing and drove over and spirited me away. Annoyed, that's a mild way of describing her mood; she was pissed off, I could tell, and didn't say a word to me as we drove home in the dark.

Of course, it was my mother who felt like a prisoner. What did she do after she dropped me off at school? How did she spend her days? Once I came home early and she was sitting at the formica table in the kitchen alcove where we sometimes ate dinner drinking Glenlivet and watching a soap opera on our small black-and-white portable. Her legs were crossed and she was brushing her hair straight downward, separating the strands with her fingers and inspecting the split ends, pausing only long enough to sip from her glass. She looked like she had been expecting a visitor who had never arrived. Someone who had promised to arrive and had changed his plans at the last minute. She didn't even get up to greet me when I walked through the door. She looked dazed, preoccupied. The people on the TV were murmuring into each other's ears. I stopped to watch and saw a man slam a door and another woman slap another woman's face because she had slept (no doubt) with her husband.

For my mother, the glass of whiskey and the TV were just props. I was a prop, really. She barely noticed me.

At night I could hear them talking, my mother and father, their room was right across the hall. I could hear my mother crying late into the night, what sounded like someone trying to muffle a cry, and then my father's voice escalating in anger until it resembled the voice of an animal caught in a trap. The cry of an animal. A howling sound, almost, like the wind makes when it pushes the branch of a tree against a closed window. It was the sound of an emotion held back. A muffled cry, as if the animal in the trap knew it was going to die.

My mother wanted to move back to the city. Anywhere but here, I could hear her say. The fucking suburbs. I'm a fucking suburban housewife. She hated the other women who were married to the other members of the faculty. She hated going to faculty parties and congregating on the periphery with the other wives. She hated being identified as someone else's wife.

We were in a café, just you and I and two other women, and we were talking about Rilke and Brecht and Goethe, as always, these were your favorite writers, and someone said: Akhmatova—have you read Anna Akhmatova? Apparently a new translation of her poems had just appeared. And I shook my head, no, I'd never even heard of her. It was the only time you ever touched me, really, in the physical sense, and maybe that's why I remember this moment so clearly. We were talking about Akhmatova and you put your hand on my arm. I was sitting next to you, we were crowded around a small table, smoking and drinking iced cappuccinos, our shoulders practically touching. I was wearing a white short-sleeved turtleneck and cutoffs. You kept your hand on my bare arm as you talked to us about Russian poetry. You acted as if you weren't aware of your fingers on my arm. That it was natural for you to be touching me in this way. You were telling us the names of all the great 20th-century Russian writers: Mayakovsky, Tsvetaeva, Mandelstam, Akhmatova, Pasternak. How I had to read them. And Khlebnikov. This last name made you laugh. "Wait till you read Khlebnikov," you said. You could speak Russian as well as German. I would have gone to bed with you that night if you had wanted. If you had made a move.

My mother used to eat all the food from my father's plate. We'd go to restaurants and she'd claim she wasn't hungry. She'd study the menu, close it, and stare into space while my father and I ordered. "Water, just water," she'd say to the waiter. And then when my father's food arrived he asked her if she wanted a taste. She stared at him, indifferent, as if the last thing she wanted was to eat his food. Deprive him of yet another pleasure. "O.K.," she said finally. "Just a small bite." As if she was doing him a big favor. As if she was honoring him by eating his food. "That's not bad," she said. She appropriated a tiny butter plate, stacking the pads of butter onto the tablecloth, and transferred the food from my father's plate onto her own. My father never even sighed. He didn't admonish her or complain. She was cutting away at his food now, taking the best pieces, sipping from his wineglass. We ate in silence, trying to blend in. An ordinary family. Just the notion of family is the ultimate in ordinariness. One can't escape from the notion of family. If we have a family we generally take it for granted or deny its existence. People whose parents are dead envy people whose parents are alive. There are endless generalities and clichés relating to family—"each unhappy family" (a familiar quote) "is unhappy in its own way"—and all of them are true. I wanted to laugh at the way my mother was acting, but I felt sorry for my father as well. How could he stand it? I was only eight years old and I remember having the barely conscious thought that I would never be able to live with someone who behaved like my mother. "Here, have some more," my father said. He pushed his plate in her direction. Maybe he was thinking that at least we were saving some money. Three meals for the price of two. And maybe he wasn't that hungry anyway.

The photograph had been taken on the balcony of their hotel room in Santa Monica. She was leaning back again the silver rails. There was sky and water in the distance, all one color, two shades of blue melting into one another. Her arms were very brown from lying in the sun all day, and the skin on her back was peeling. Obviously, the lotion she was using to protect her skin wasn't strong enough.

Dean hated the beach. Even on the hottest days he wore a denim jacket over his long-sleeved shirt.

She had been sitting in the chair on the balcony smoking a cigarette and drinking a cup of instant coffee. It was ten in the morning and she'd been awake for hours. Escaping into books again, this time Henry James's *The Wings of the Dove*, which she'd read in college but had forgotten.

She always had a hard time sleeping when she visited a new place.

Dean had appeared at the door of the balcony, naked, and told her to turn around. He had snapped the photograph and they had gone inside and fucked until it was time for him to leave for a business meeting.

"I'll be back for dinner," he had said. It was what he always said when he left her for the day. When she kissed him goodbye she could feel the gun in his shoulder holster.

Once, when she asked him how things were going, he turned to her and said: "You don't want to know."

One day you were lecturing to us about Rilke's *Elegies*. And the next week you were gone. There was the chairman of the department announcing to the class that you were gone and that he was going to replace you until the end of the semester. There was no explanation, though everyone knew you'd been fired for sleeping with one of your students. What we didn't know, of course, was that this had happened to you before, at your previous job at a college in California. That you had been fired from a previous job for the same reason and that the only reason you had been hired by New York University was because you knew the chairman. He was a friend of yours, but he couldn't help you now. He had warned you that such a thing might some day happen. Sexual harassment was a big deal. Every day there was an article in the newspaper about an incident of harassment involving a secretary and her boss or a senator who slept with all his assistants. You knew the risk involved but you did it anyway. You could say, in your own defense, that you didn't coerce anyone to do something they didn't want to do. That the students you slept with were adults. But it didn't matter.

It wasn't long after you were fired that I met Dean, the movie producer, and a year later I moved into his townhouse on East 62nd Street. Dean offered to support me while I finished my dissertation on Akhmatova, but what I really wanted to do was write a novel. Stories. I had begun writing stories while I was an undergraduate. I had a collection of stories and the first chapters of a novel. An agent (someone I met through Dean) was interested, but had no luck selling it (so far). Sometimes my confidence was high, anything seemed possible; other days, I was tempted to burn everything I'd written and start anew. Dean had projects in Los Angeles and Paris and was gone a good deal of the time. It was a marriage of convenience, in a way. We rarely had sex. I knew he had girlfriends in other cities, but I didn't say anything.

Twice a week, when he was at home, I organized dinner parties for other producers and actors and screen writers. It was at one of these parties that I met Elizabeth Taylor. Dean had produced one of her movies and they had other friends in common. It was there that I met Vince, who worked for the Mayor's office, and was an old friend of Elizabeth's. He had helped her raise money for AIDS research, one of her many causes. But it wasn't until a year later that Vince and I met again and became lovers. Once a week in room 19 on the 3rd floor of the Hotel Albert on 10th Street and University. We met once a week, spoke on the phone in between, but on this particular afternoon he didn't appear. He had dropped by earlier in the day and left a message: "I'll see you next week." The man behind the desk looked worried as he handed me the note. I had seen this man once a week for six months but we had never exchanged a word. (Later, after Vincent's body had been discovered in a dump on Staten Island, the police would question the man from the hotel, show him pictures of me and Vince, and he would tell them everything.) I walked into the sunlight, the note folded into the palm of my hand, and headed east to St. Mark's Place, to the café opposite your apartment. I can't deny that I felt disappointed at not being able to see Vince. I'd be a liar if I said that my life didn't revolve around the hours that we spent together. I imagined the room—we met in the same room every week—with the paint flaking from the ceiling. The window of the room looked out over an alleyway behind the hotel. A flamenco dancer in spiked heels was practicing in the room above us. The mattress had a valley in the center. I could see both of us, as if through a keyhole, Vincent pulling my hair as he came at me from behind. I was sitting at the table in the café, writing in my notebook. This is what I was doing when I saw you on the street.

I used to lie awake thinking of killing Carl. I was still young enough to believe that the man is always the coercive force in a relationship. That it was Carl who seduced my mother, that it was he who wrecked my parents' marriage. Sometimes I think it's best to live by a code: don't get involved with anyone who's married or living with someone else. I'm not saying that doing such a thing is easy, but it's something to keep in mind. I don't remember when it occurred to me that my mother might have been at least partially at fault. That it was she who had seduced Carl, not the other way around. It was she who pursued him, who went to his apartment after his lecture. Carl himself was getting over a bad first marriage. He had been living alone for two years and was ready, in a sense, for my mother's version of intimacy, which was like being eaten alive. My mother is a consumer. A devourer, a reciprocator, a giver, a sharer. She believes in codependency. She was never just content with living together—that was only part of it. She was uncomfortable when the process of giving and taking wasn't flowing smoothly, or when it wasn't flowing at all. If you were reading a book you had to talk about what you were reading literally while you were doing it, so that meant you had to experience and communicate your experience simultaneously. It's like announcing, five minutes after you arrive at a party, that "this is a great party." She would read the introductions to books, the first chapters, and stop there. She was often reading four or five books simultaneously. Her sense of devouring involved quantity, bits and pieces of as many people and things as possible. She knew that she was risking her marriage to my father by going off with Carl, that eventually my father would find out. She wanted him to find out. He refused to admit to himself that it was happening until it was too late. She kept intending to tell him, but preferred to lie instead. Maybe I don't give them enough credit; maybe Carl should get a medal. It's been twenty years since my father tried to kill them, and they're still together.

We met at a party. It was the first party Dean and I gave after I moved into his house. Dean liked to have people over when he was in town, and it was my job to call people up and to arrange for a cook to come on the day of the party and prepare the food. There was a Haitian woman named Marlene who was the regular cook and her niece Claudette came twice a week to clean the house.

Vince and I sat opposite one another at the long dining room table. I remember that he kept looking at me incredulously, as if he couldn't understand why I had married someone like Dean, a person twice my age. I remember talking to him about his job, but I don't remember his exact words. We didn't get together until almost a year later.

It was at another party, the penthouse apartment of a TV director on the Upper East Side, about ten blocks north of where I was living with Dean. We were standing on the balcony smoking. Dean was in Paris making some deal on a new movie, lining up a director and fucking whoever he fucked when he went to Paris. The first thing Dean asked when he came back from one of his trips was whether I'd fucked anyone while he was gone. I said "no" because it was true but I knew I would lie if it wasn't.

"Do you remember Vince?" someone said, as a way of introducing us.

We were alone on the balcony, staring at the city fifty stories below. It was midsummer and I was wearing a sleeveless print dress with straps crisscrossing my back and he was wearing a shirt with the sleeves rolled up and black jeans with an alligator belt. It was after midnight but not much cooler than it had been during the day, maybe ninety degrees, the middle of a heat wave. Vince was tall and spindly and melancholy looking in contrast to Dean, who was smaller than I was and always smiling. Vince put his hand out behind me in a way that made me think he was going to put his arm around my bare shoulders or touch my back with his fingertips. But then he managed to move around me without touching. He was pointing at a star directly above the World Trade Towers. He said he used to live in the country and could name all the constellations but since he moved to New York he never even looked at the sky.

"How's your husband?" he asked, pretending not to remember Dean's name.

"Out of town," I said.

"Do you like being alone?"

I wondered why Vince was never invited to any of the subsequent parties that Dean and I gave and then I realized it was because Dean had been jealous of him for talking to me during dinner. Most of the men who attended our parties steered clear of me, other than to thank me for inviting them (if even that), since they knew that the slightest hint of intimacy would make Dean jealous. The last thing anyone wanted was to be the object of Dean's anger. As always, when we were in a crowded room, I felt Dean was watching me, even when he was talking to someone else.

Vince had been taking a chance when he talked to me at that first party. Maybe he was just dumb, or didn't care.

I knew there were people at the TV director's house who knew Dean and who might report back to him that I had spent time talking with Vince. I wasn't even supposed to leave the house when Dean was away, much less go to a party by myself.

Before meeting Dean I went to parties where all everyone talked about were the books they were reading or the dissertations they were writing or the courses they were taking or the teaching jobs that were available. But Dean's friends never read books. They read scripts. They talked about "properties." Other people read books and told them that these books might make good movies. Then they read a quick summary of the books, two or three pages at most. Or, if it was really good, a first chapter. They would pay a writer fifty thousand dollars for the rights to a property that might or might not ever be translated into a movie that anyone would see.

Sometimes when the option ran out they'd pay another fifty thousand just so no one else would get interested and make the movie.

Most of the movies lost millions of dollars. Dean was involved with the money end, the hiring and firing, the choosing. He had power over the people who made the choices. He kept a gun in his desk drawer and another in the drawer of the table on the side of our bed. And sometimes, when we kissed goodbye, I could feel the bulge of a gun under his coat.

Vince was different from most of the men who

showed up at our parties. Most of them were out-of-towners, parasites from Los Angeles or Las Vegas. Occasionally a European type with pointed shoes would kiss me on both cheeks when we said goodbye. Vince worked in politics, he was an aide to the mayor, a member of the State Arts Council, something official. The reason he had been invited to the party had to do with money. If you wanted to make a movie in New York, Vince could tell you who had the money to give. If Vince approved of a film project, half the battle was won.

But mostly, he had been invited because he was a friend of Elizabeth's. Not a lover, but a friend. "He's one of my dearest friends," she told me at the party. She had insisted that he come.

I want to remember everything we said to one another in the time that we were together. There was something unclear about it all even when it was happening, and sometimes I had the feeling you weren't even listening to me when I spoke. Sometimes, in the early days, after Vincent was murdered, when I was still hiding out from everyone, I would lie awake at dawn, watching you sleep, and think: is that what I waited for all these years? Is this what I want? As always, I was being hard on myself, and another voice would always respond to the first, like participants in a Socratic dialogue, and beg me to appreciate what I already had. I had heard that voice before: it was my mother. It was Dean. I knew that once I had something I really wanted I was invariably dissatisfied and wanted something else, that this was my nature, my inheritance, possibly, the idea that simply taking pleasure in the largesse of what had been given to me was like dying. The pleasure of loving you from a distance was different from the reality of actually being with you, but this is true of everything. No one's perfect—is it necessary for me to say this? All relationships have their unique set of problems. It was I who was creating the problem by surrounding our life with a litany of needs and wants that would eventually lead me astray, until the person who had loved you from a distance had disappeared. That's why I want to catch it all now. Because this book isn't about you.

"I can't tell you how many times I've replayed that day in my head. Every Sunday that fall my father and I drove to the Palisades in the used Mercedes he had bought in Vermont the summer before. We had a favorite place, we had discovered it accidentally, where we could walk up a winding path to a hill overlooking the Hudson. I don't know when my father realized that my mother was spending her free afternoons with her lover Carl, the famous journalist who had just arrived a few weeks before to lecture at the college for a year. He had given a talk one night on campus, something about photojournalism, which she had attended, and I guess she had been impressed enough to go for a drink with him afterward, she and some other people, and of course he had singled her out because he knew instinctively that she would be the easiest to seduce (you could read the desperation in her eyes), that of all the women in the room he could go to bed with, she was the one most in need of a change. I don't know whether my father knew that she was seeing him during the week as well as on Sunday. Every time either of them had two free hours they would meet in the condominium he was renting for a year and have sex. How did they do it? I imagine them leaning up against the kitchen table or against the stove. I can't imagine my parents making love, but I can imagine my mother and Carl.

The house was always empty when my father and I returned from our trips, but my mother was always home before dinnertime. That afternoon, when we drove to the country, I knew something was wrong. I can't say I didn't realize something was wrong before that day but I preferred not to think about it. I had my own life, after all. I was ten years old."

They met once a week in the hotel on Tenth Street, whether Dean was in town or not. When he was around, she could always make up some excuse for going out. She became good at telling lies which were simple declarative statements describing an imaginary reality. When Dean was away on business, she and Vincent spoke on the phone every night. She assumed, early in their life together, that Dean had hired someone to follow her, that he himself was embroidering a parallel reality of lies and subterfuge, pretending to believe her when of course he knew exactly where she was going and whom she was seeing. Once, when she was leaving the hotel, she saw a man with a white t-shirt and dreadlocks back into a doorway across the street. Another time it was a middle-aged man with a moustache and a beret. She stopped to look in a store window and he stopped too. She imagined men with submachine guns stationed on the roof of the building across from the hotel who were reporting to Dean via beepers and cell phones about her comings and goings. She imagined that the room where she and Vincent met twice a week was bugged. They met in the same room every time. "I'm going shopping," she said to Dean. He looked up from what he was doing as if he was too busy to care. "Have a good time," he said. And then he smiled.

I remember—right after I registered for your class—this woman, I forget her name—I told her the name of the teacher—you—I told her you were teaching the course—and she looked at me, she said: Be careful, he likes women—he seduces all his women students—And I remember thinking: All of them? How could that be possible? And not only that, not only did you seduce your students—that's what she said—but they fell in love with you—You were like their fathers, that's how they thought of you—A typical relationship: teacher/father—All men with authority take on that role, don't you think? It was too easy to make that connection—I tried not to think of you that way—I watched the way you stared at all the women in the class—There was a rumor that you were sleeping with this woman named Margaret—She had taken your class before—I remember thinking she wasn't very pretty—I couldn't understand why you were interested in her, you could have anyone—There were eight women in the class, only two men—We were all waiting for you to make your move, to call us into your office, to ask us for lunch—I would have gone with you anywhere, then, I was willing, if you had only looked at me—And then mid-semester we heard the news: you were being forced to leave—This woman had fallen in love with you and you refused to sleep with her—You had slept together once and now you wanted to end it—That's what everyone said—And she was getting back at you—She accused you of raping her—You had taken advantage of your position—I'm just telling you what everyone said.

You didn't realize that getting fired for sleeping with one of your students was really a blessing in disguise. You had become bitter and frustrated like every other

English teacher. What you really wanted to do was write a novel. You had been planning to write a novel for years. You would tell people who didn't know you well that you were doing research for your novel. That you were taking notes. You would make dumb excuses about the difficulty of teaching and writing at the same time. You used your affairs with your students as a way of avoiding the tedium of sitting down and actually writing a book. You had become accustomed to the social aspects of being a teacher. Conversations with students. Going out with them to a bar or coffee shop after class. The last thing you wanted to do was stay at home every day. When you were teaching you were motivated by the need to impress your students, to make them fall in love with you. And now that you were no longer teaching you had something to prove as well. There had been articles in the *New York Times* and *The Village Voice* about your history as a seducer of students. The articles seemed to hint that the woman named Margaret was telling the truth when she said you had raped her. "Rape" was the word she had used. You tried to defend yourself but no one wanted to hear your version; no one except your other students. You could say that she had made love willingly, that she was accusing you of being a rapist as a way of getting back at you because you didn't want to continue the affair, but most people would be prejudiced against you for even contemplating the idea of sleeping with one of your students. It was against the code, the so-called moral code, that seems to insist that a teacher has psychological power over his or her students. That it's a way of taking advantage of someone with less power than you. That there's no way to give someone a fair grade if that person is your lover. And if you don't give an A to the person you've slept with? She'll accuse you of rape, of course. No one realized how vulnerable you were (not even your colleagues, who probably fooled around with their students as well, or wanted to, and were simply jealous because you had actually taken the risk). And none of the students you had slept with in the past came forward to accuse you of harassment or rape. No one came forth to defend you either, but there was no reason to do this. Just the fact that you had fucked one of your students made you guilty in most people's eyes. So now you had no excuse. You had an idea for a novel. You were living in the apartment on St. Marks Place, between First Avenue and Avenue A, where you're living now. Some days you didn't even go outside. You worked on a typewriter, an old IBM. You woke at noon, drank coffee, read the *Times,* and then went to work. Some days you would sit at your desk for ten or twelve hours at a stretch. You had an idea for a novel, and now it was just a matter of inching your way from page to page. When you weren't at your desk you were taking notes about your characters. You listened to jazz because your main character, a detective, was a jazz aficionado. Fifties jazz, mostly. Early Miles, Coltrane, Monk. Bill Evans. And Russia. You were writing a novel about a detective who falls in love with a Russian woman while investigating the murder of a prostitute. So you read books about Russia, you even thought of going to Russia, but it never happened. It wasn't necessary. The character of the Russian woman was actually based on one of your old students. Someone you'd slept with, of course, but only once.

As soon as I started seeing Vince I knew my life with Dean was doomed. We had been married a little more than a year but I knew I had made a mistake. He was gone at least half of every month, and when he was home we rarely saw one another. He seemed to have lost interest in sex, at least with me. In the pockets of his jackets I found scraps of paper with names like Simone or Juliette, along with phone numbers, and I assumed that these were the women he was sleeping with when he went to Paris. "I'm going to Paris next week," he would announce. He kept his business deals to himself; he assumed, from the early days of our life together, that I wouldn't be interested. Sometimes he flew to Los Angeles and stayed one night and then returned the next day. He always called me, every night, when he was away, but not so much to find out how I had spent my day, or because he cared about me, but because he wanted to make sure I was being faithful to him. He made it clear that if I wasn't home when he called, usually after midnight, there would be trouble.

It was two in the morning on the night that Vince walked me home from the party.

Fifteen minutes after we walked in the door I was sitting in the chair in the living room and Vince was going down on me, my legs resting on his shoulders. It was something Dean rarely did, not even in the beginning of our relationship. Vince slipped his fingers inside me, his tongue moving between my legs. For a moment that seemed to last indefinitely, I thought I was going to faint, or fall off the chair. When the phone rang (there are three phones in the house, one in the bedroom, another in the kitchen, yet another in Dean's office), I didn't tell Vince to stop even though we both knew who was calling, that only one person would be calling at 2:15 A.M., that he'd probably called before (I hadn't checked the machine).

"Don't," I said to Vince, as he lifted his head.

I pressed my thighs together, grabbing handfuls of his hair, squeezing his head between my legs like a vise.

I cried out in pleasure until the phone stopped ringing.

If it wasn't for you—talking about Rilke as you did that night—first in class, then in the café afterward where you always went, surrounded by adoring students—this is before the woman named Margaret accused you of raping her—everyone knew she was lying—Even before I entered the class I knew your reputation—that you slept with your students—And I remember feeling hurt—that you weren't attracted to me—I remember waiting for some sign from you—some recognition—but it never happened. There's a light on at your window every time I walk by at night. Sometimes, late at night—two, three in the morning—you're still at your desk. I rehearse in my mind what I might say if we ever met. I wonder if you'll remember me. We only went out once together, but it was in a group—five or six women, two guys, and you—after class. We went to a coffee shop near the university. It was listening to you talk that I realized the difference between knowing something and being familiar with something. You spoke about the things you knew as if they were part of your being, not something memorized, while everything I ever read passed through me, like the memory of a dream. Until I met you, I never understood what I was reading.

At one point, as we sat around the table in the coffee shop, you touched my arm and said: "Akhmatova? Have you ever read her?" And I blushed. It was my moment to impress you, but I couldn't say anything. You wrote her name on a napkin, which I still have, and the next day I went to the bookstore and bought a copy of Akhmatova's *Collected Poems*. Took a biography of her out from the library. It suddenly occurred to me that the best way to impress someone is to know everything. The next time we met, I vowed to myself, I'd be ready.

You had saved enough money to take a year off. You gave yourself a year. It would take that long to finish your novel. "I was a hermit," is how you described it. We were lying in bed and you were describing the year after you were fired. "I didn't see anyone," you said. "I didn't sleep with anyone either." I told you about the time before I met Dean, when I was celibate for three years, but I wondered if you were listening. Sometimes, after I finished telling you a story out of my past, you would look at me with a blank expression as if you hadn't heard a word. "I'm sorry," you said. "I was thinking about my book."

By the time we met on the street you were already writing your second novel. You had sold the first one— even before you had finished it—for a hundred thousand dollars. I read it, of course; it was what inspired me to write a book of my own. Not because your book was anything great, but because I knew that being a writer might be one way to impress you. I had fantasies of writing a book, selling it to a publisher and then to the movies, and then meeting you at a party. You would say: "I read your book," and I would remind you that you had once been my teacher. That you were my teacher before I was famous. "You taught me everything I know," I would say.

The second novel, this was your problem. "It's going badly," were your words when we met outside your building. I was sitting at the window of my favorite coffeehouse on St. Mark's Place when I saw you coming from a distance. I had been sitting at my usual table near the window, pretending to read, but this particular afternoon in mid-June I wasn't even pretending. I was staring at the staircase leading up to the front door of your building. It was just an ordinary tenement, with a steep staircase and wrought-iron bannisters. I was thinking of your first novel, and the Russian woman Marina, because there was a woman who looked Russian sitting at a table across from me who kept staring at me. What everyone liked about your book was the relationship between the detective and the Russian woman; it was more like a love story, the reviewers said, than a detective novel. That was the flaw, if anything. No one cared about the murder of the dead prostitute, Yvonne de Marco, but the sex scenes between Marina and the detective were what made the book special. There was some talk that people in Hollywood might be interested; I even gave a copy to Dean, my husband, but I don't think he even read it. I was thinking about all these things when I saw you coming. In jeans and t-shirt (it was ninety five degrees), a black shoulder bag. And me, in my thin blouse and skirt, ran into the street, leaving my book bag behind, leaving my half-filled glass of iced coffee behind, leaving my imaginary world behind. This was real, this was you. I saw you coming, I stood up so suddenly the table shook and the coffee spilled over the edges of the glass. The ice cubes rattled in the glass. I pushed back my chair and ran into the street to meet you.

ENDLESS EMBRACE

A PLACE IN THE SUN

1

There was a rumor when I was in high school that a girl named Bettina invited boys back to her house during lunch hour and after school. She would sit on the side of her bed, wearing only a bathrobe, and allow one boy at a time to touch her breasts and place his fingers inside her. That's all she let them do. After the boys took their turns (fifteen minutes each), they would wait in the living room, drinking beer and tossing the empty cans out the window. That's how she was discovered: the neighbors complained about the loud music and the bottles and cans crashing to the pavement in the middle of the afternoon. Bettina's parents were called in by the school principal, Bettina denied everything but was expelled anyway, and her family moved to another part of the city. All the boys involved went unpunished: they bragged that they had fucked her, of course, but I know this wasn't true.

2

Pepper told me he was gay on the train from Boston to New York. I had said something about the woman sitting a few rows ahead of us. She walked down the aisle to the bathroom and caught my eye, a flicker of contact, of mutual interest, accompanied by a vague come-and-get-me smile. When she returned to her seat she crossed her legs and swung them out into the aisle and glanced back at me with a kind of longing that indicated we were thinking the same thing. She was sitting alone and I asked Pepper if he minded if I deserted him for awhile.

"For her?" he asked, petulant, then shrugged. "If that's what you like."

I'd never met anyone on a train before but I'd had fantasies about sitting next to a stranger in the dark while the train rattled over the Alps, our coats blanketing our knees and thighs, hands fumbling with zippers until they alighted on bare skin. I'd fallen asleep inside that dream more than once and now it seemed like a possibility. When I was younger I'd always been too shy to make the first move, but now I had no time to despair about being rejected. I'd flagellated myself too often in the past over lost chances of making contact with women I was attracted to. All you can do is try, and if they cut you down, no problem; you can walk away with your ego in one piece. If it works once in a hundred times it's worth it, don't you think?

But Pepper held my attention, wouldn't let me go. He acted like he was disappointed in me for preferring the woman's company to his.

"And you?" I asked. "What's your pleasure?"

He looked surprised. I guess he thought that everyone

knew he was gay. It wasn't like he'd kept it a secret. He was a close friend of my former girlfriend Lee Ann, but she had never told me he liked men and I'd never thought to ask. Lee Ann had been the last of my college girlfriends and the only one who I could imagine living with. We had actually spent a number of nights lying awake in bed talking about what it would be like sharing an apartment off-campus. But of course, as soon as we realized that we were becoming inseparable, that we were falling in love, that we woke up thinking about each other when we weren't together, we began drifting apart. We talked about living together and then we put up a wall between us to prevent it from happening.

Lee Ann had introduced me to Pepper. He was sometimes around when I visited her, sitting on the floor listening to Patsy Cline records, and he often left soon after I arrived, figuring we wanted to be alone. And it was true. For the first few months we were together we couldn't keep our hands off each other. We liked to take showers together. To fuck in the shower. We were already jaded from too much sex with other people, even though we were both only twenty-one, born only days apart in the same year, with our moons in Scorpio, so we tried to add a bit of tenderness and sweetness to the relationship to offset the pose that none of it mattered.

Pepper said: "I always thought you liked men too."

"What gave you that idea?"

"Lee Ann always said you were too sweet to be totally straight. None of her other boyfriends were that nice to her. That's what she said."

"I was trying to be sweet," I said. "I'm really not."

"I used to watch you when you were with your friends. I saw you all once in a restaurant but you didn't see me so I had a chance to observe. And what I saw—what I heard—was that you were different from them."

And then: "I think I'm in love with you. Don't be angry at me. I know it must sound crazy. Just don't sit with someone else."

He turned his head away, staring at his reflection in the window of the train, and for a moment I thought he was going to start crying. I wanted to put my arm around his shoulders in an attempt to comfort him, though I knew he would interpret the gesture as a sign that I was interested, that there was some hope, that maybe Lee Ann was right about me after all. If someone says they love you, no matter same sex or opposite, whatever your choice, it's hard to walk away. The fact that I'd never been with a man before was intriguing to me as well. I'd never even had a fantasy about a man, though most of the women I knew had experimented with other women, at least once. Most men, if they'd slept with another man, didn't talk about it much, at least not with other men. I tried to imagine what it would be like lying in bed with Pepper hovering over me. "You can do whatever you want," I would say. He was at least a half-foot shorter than I was. If we were in prison together I would be his protector, and he would be the guy who traded sex for protection. He would pretend he was a girl to please me, wear silk lingerie which he would smuggle into jail in return for giving the guard a blow job. All the while I was thinking of the woman a few rows ahead. She was probably twice my age, married or recently divorced. She would tell me her name—a false name, no doubt—and we would rent a hotel room together near Times Square.

But I was sick of living inside my fantasies. More than once, I'd led myself down a dark alleyway by thoughts which were no more than illusions, blips on a screen the size of a match head. In reality, all I knew was that I was on a train, five years of undergraduate college life behind me, sitting next to a person I didn't know well who was claiming he was in love with me.

It was time to talk in clichés.

"You only think you're in love with me," I said. "You don't really know me."

I could hear myself saying this to someone else—the same words, same tone—like an echo down the walls of a ravine. The friend of my older sister who had fallen in love with me when I was in high school. We had just fucked and I was getting dressed. Sitting on the side of her bed in her parents' apartment on Park Avenue. I was fourteen. She was telling me that she thought she was falling in love with me and that she wanted to see me the next night as well. That she would wait at home for me to call and that she would be available whenever I wanted to fuck. That my sister had been right when she told her that she would like me. I didn't understand why anyone would want to fall in love with me, or think they were in love with me, why my sister was pimping for me, or what love had to do with sex, so I didn't really believe her when she said this. She took my hand and put it between her legs. I could get an erection every ten minutes in those days and we had already made love twice in the last hour and I knew that it wasn't long before her mother came home from work. She climbed on top of me, reaching between us, putting me inside, wrapping her legs around my waist. She didn't say "fuck me, fuck me" like some of my girlfriends did, but she cried when she came, the tears streaming down her face.

It was an accident—no, coincidence—that I was taking this trip with Pepper. My friend Derrick, who had graduated the year before, had promised to drive up and bring me back to the city. I had boxes of books, a computer, all the term papers I had written in the last five years, a carton of CDs. He was going to borrow his stepfather's car and take me home, but the night before Derrick's mother had discovered that Derrick's stepfather had lost a thousand dollars betting on the Utah-Chicago basketball playoffs and she had kicked him out. It wasn't the first time Derrick's stepfather had bet on a sporting event and lost, and Derrick's mother had a good argument against him since the money he was betting with was hers by inheritance and this jerk she had married hadn't worked a day in the five years they had known each other. Her friends had been advising her to kick him out since day one and she finally did it, this was the last straw, and as a consequence he needed the car, really Derrick's mother's car which she had bought him, to transport himself and his belongings to temporary living quarters. Derrick called me the night before and told me all this and I found a place to store my things, the basement of the house of my Russian language teacher, Professor Roshenko. All I was taking with me on the train ride was my laptop and my shoulder bag filled with books.

I didn't run into Pepper until I'd arrived at the train station and bought my ticket.

"I'm not supposed to be here," I said.

"Nor am I. My ride fell through."

"So what are we going to do? Sit together in silence? Make small talk? Try to think of things to say?"

"It won't be that difficult," he said. "We have more in common than you think."

"The only thing we have in common is my ex-girlfriend Lee Ann."

"That, and more."

Halfway into the trip, after he confessed that he was secretly in love with me, "ever since I first met you," he said, which dates back almost a year, he also confessed that it was no real accident that we had met at the station.

I had called Lee Ann the night before to say goodbye—she had another year of prison before graduation—and he had been in her apartment. He had heard, or she had told him, about my change of plans, that I was returning to the city on the train the next day. He had been planning to leave a day later, but it was worth it to him to change his schedule so he could spend four hours alone with me.

"Does Lee Ann know how you feel?"

"Of course she does. She told me to tell you."

"How did she think I was going to respond?"

"She didn't know. She said she had a theory that you liked men as well. That you went both ways. That you refused to admit it but it was true."

"Anything is possible," I said, relieved that we had something to talk about.

The blonde woman two rows ahead glanced back again, losing hope.

"Do you think we'll ever see each other again when we get off this train?"

"Of course we will. I have your friend Derrick's phone number, where you'll be staying."

"So what? You'll call me up? You'll stand outside the building?"

"Whatever it takes," Pepper said, a man with a mission. "I know you want to see me and that it's just a matter of being patient on my part. I'm good at waiting."

"Just because I tried to be nice to Lee Ann doesn't mean I'm queer."

"According to Lee Ann, all the other guys she went out with before you had one thing on their minds. And all they did, in the long run, was fuck her over. That's what guys do to women. But you—you wanted to take a shower with her. You wanted to hold hands. You wanted to talk about your feelings."

"I didn't have any feelings," I said. "There was nothing to talk about."

Pepper put his hand on my knee.

"Your hand is on my knee," I said.

"It's just a hand, I'm just a person like everyone else."

I didn't get his point, but I didn't push him away, or slap his face, as a woman once did to me in a crowded movie theater when I tried to put my hand down the front of her blouse. I wondered if the people sitting in front or behind us could hear our conversation.

The only person I ever talk to about sex is Derrick, whom I've known since highschool, and we never talk about sex with men. There are some things I've never told anyone, not even Derrick, not even my therapist, certainly not any of my women lovers, and never my parents, who are divorced and live in California and didn't even bother to show up for my graduation.

It was raining, finally, and the haze was melting over the distant factories of some east coast city that had outlived its usefulness as a hub of capitalism and was just spouting thick halos of smoke into the invisible sky for no purpose.

I put my hand over his hand and moved it from my knee to the inside of my thigh.

"There's hope," he said.

"I have an erection," I said. "When I think that I could be sitting with that woman I get excited."

"You can think about anything. You can have fantasies about anyone you want. I do it better than any woman you've ever been with. Better than Lee Ann."

I pushed him away. Reached into my book bag for a sweater and draped it over my stomach. Unzipped my jeans.

"Do it with your hand," I said. "I'll give you five minutes."

3

I was lying in bed with a woman much older than myself when a branch began moving against the window, scratching at it, so that unexpectedly in the course of having sex I assumed that the sound of the branch against the glass was a signal that the woman's husband was returning home. It was only weeks later, when the husband somehow learned that his wife and I were sleeping together, that I heard (late one night) the sound of his footsteps beneath my window, the scratching of a branch against the glass, and the voice of someone too drunk to do anything but stand beneath my window and call out my name.

4

His name was Nelson Lindegaard, and he was heading back to Florida to see his wife and daughter. He hadn't seen them in more than a year and they didn't know he was coming. He and his wife Nicole had been married by the justice of the peace in the courthouse in Tampa when they were both sixteen. He had dropped out of high school at the end of his junior year and found a job in an Amoco station in Tampa. He wanted to train as a mechanic but he spent most of his time feeding gas into the cars of people who didn't even look him in the face or say thank you. His daughter Esta was born a year later. Most people assumed the reason Nelson and Nicole married so young was because Nicole was already pregnant, but it wasn't true. At the Amoco station he earned $4.50 an hour, not enough to support his new family, so he began selling guns. Handguns, magnums, semiautomatic shotguns, hunting rifles. There was a cabin in the woods behind the gas station which he used to store the weapons. He was the middle man, but he managed to make three times the amount he earned at the station, enough to buy Nicole some of the things she coveted, mostly clothing.

He had purposely requested the all-night shift at the gas station so he could do his business with the guns when no one was around. It was the only station open all night in a twenty-five-mile radius but there weren't too many cars around at four in the morning and he had plenty of time to carry on his gun business and to sit back at the desk in the office and imagine Nicole modeling the red dress he had bought for her the day before, unzipping it, shrugging it off her shoulders, as he sat back and watched. He had told the owners of the station that he was nineteen and they assumed he could handle the night shift on his own.

Nicole appreciated the extra money, she knew about the guns, but she hated sleeping alone. She hated *being* alone, even for a few minutes; if they didn't have a baby she'd probably spend most of her nights hanging out with Nelson at the station. Sleeping on a futon on the floor was better than sleeping alone in the king sized bed, the empty space beside her a reminder of her own mortality. With Nelson she forgot about dying, at least for the moment. A baby sleeping in the next room wasn't the company she needed. And all Nelson ever did when he came home from work was fall asleep. He rarely even played with the baby, except in the evenings before she went to bed. He would arrive home at dawn and sleep till late in the afternoon, which meant that Nicole was responsible for taking care of the baby during the day and entertaining herself at night. The only time Nicole had a breather from taking care of the baby was after dinner when Nelson turned on the stereo and danced her around the room. "Blue, blue, blue suede shoes," he would coo in her ear, tilting the baby's head back to make her laugh. The only time she and Nelson made love was in the evenings after Esta was asleep. And then, instead of falling asleep together, he had to get out of bed and go to work.

There was a rumor, and Nelson was the first to hear it, that Nicole had a boyfriend, that she was sleeping with someone when he was at the gas station. Nelson didn't bother to ask Nicole whether the rumor was true. He found out the name of the suspected boyfriend, Harold Warner, and learned that he was the manager of a 7-Eleven about a mile from the Amoco station, that he closed up the store at ten, ate dinner somewhere or had a drink, and then headed off to see Nicole. Not every night, but maybe twice, three times a week.

One night Nelson told Nicole that he had to go to work a few hours earlier than usual. He drove to the 7-Eleven and parked out back and waited until Harold Warner had closed up. He waited in the woods behind the store until Harold Warner locked the door behind him and was walking across the deserted parking lot to his Honda Civic. Nelson's own car was parked in the lot but Harold Warner didn't notice it or think it was suspicious. Whose car could it be, anyway? Obviously Harold Warner was thinking about something else. Nelson stepped out from behind a tree and walked around to the driver's side of the Honda and placed the barrel of the gun against the side of Harold Warner's neck and told him to turn out the lights of the car and follow him.

"What's all this about?" Harold asked.

They walked into the woods behind the Seven-Eleven,

deep enough so they could no longer see the lights from the highway. Instead of the hum of cars going by they could hear the sound of branches swaying in the wind. What sounded like an owl in the top of a tree.

"I have a question to ask you," Nelson said. "If you answer truthfully you'll be all right. If you lie, I'll have to kill you. Do you understand?"

Harold was a scrawny six feet with a bad case of acne and unwashed dirty brown hair that curled over one eye. Not very pleasant to look at, Nelson thought, and not exactly Nicole's type. Nicole liked men who were interested in clothing, in "looking nice," and Harold Warner was wearing a plain white shirt and baggy trousers with cuffs and pleats, the kind Nicole hated, or so she said. It occurred to Nelson that maybe he was talking to the wrong man. He asked Harold Warner if he knew who he was and Harold said he didn't and then Nelson asked him if he knew Nicole Lindegaard, maiden name Rodriguez, and Harold paused long enough to make Nelson think that not only did he know who he was talking about, he was fucking her when he got off from work just like everyone said. But he wanted to hear Nelson say it.

"Are you fooling around with Nicole Lindegaard?" he asked. "Remember, I'll know if you're lying. Don't ask me how I'll know but I'll know."

He walked backward, one step at a time, until he was about twenty feet from the suspected adulterer.

"You know what they do in Iran if they catch

someone stealing?" he said, pointing the gun at Harold's chest. "You know what the punishment is? I heard it on the radio. They cut off your hand, that's what. Pretty serious business. What do you think they do if they catch someone sleeping with another man's wife? What do you think they cut off then?"

He shot Harold Warner twice, once in the left thigh and once in the right foot, and walked back to the 7-Eleven parking lot and got into his car and drove home. Nicole was sitting in the living room, wearing a red nightgown, drinking a wine cooler and watching *The Breakfast Club* on the VCR. He told her that he just shot her boyfriend, not mentioning his name, and that he was going to leave town. If the cops asked where he was or if any of his business acquaintances (she knew he meant the people who bought guns) asked what had happened to him, she should tell them that he was visiting his mother in North Carolina. He wasn't sure whether Harold was going to tell the cops, but he couldn't take any chances either. The last thing he wanted was to end up in jail. He packed his duffel bag with sweaters, shirts, underwear, and socks and tossed it into the trunk of his 1985 Ford, which he had bought for $1,250 at Albie's Used Car Lot in St. Petersburg last year. He had a thousand dollars cash from selling guns, but he didn't know a person in the world who lived outside of Tampa with whom he could stay until it was safe to return. If it was ever safe. He couldn't even look at Nicole, in her red nightgown, who sat on the living room sofa all the while he was upstairs packing, not saying anything for fear that it might make him more angry than he already was. Seeing her in the nightgown, which he had bought her on their third wedding anniversary, was almost as bad as finding her in bed with her lover. Before leaving the house he called the hospital in downtown Tampa and told the woman who answered the phone that there was a wounded man in the woods behind the 7-Eleven on Route 9. The last thing he wanted was for Harold to die. Killing him wasn't the point. Now that he had shot him, he no longer cared what Harold and Nicole did together. If he thought too much about it he would get sick and then he might have to do something to Nicole as well. He drove into the night, without even kissing his daughter goodbye, and when he was too tired to drive he pulled the car down a dead-end road and dozed off for an hour, stretched out on the front seat. Whenever he stopped for gas he bought a Coke from a machine, then went into the bathroom in the back of the gas station to wash his face and swallow a handful of diet pills to keep him going until he reached New York, a place where he had never been. I'll get a room in a hotel. I'll get a job. He would call up Nicole after a few months and not say anything. Listen to the sound of her voice on the other end of the line, her breathing, and then hang up.

5

It was ten o'clock, a Sunday night, the end of July, during a summer when people all over the country were dying of the heat, when cows were toppling over, when old people who didn't know enough to open their windows were suffocating in their sleep. It was remarkable, or maybe not (why should anything shock me?), that so many people were living in isolation, no family or friends, not even a neighbor to inquire whether they needed a glass of water. People were dying from lack of love, or too much of it. A woman in the south had killed her two young children because her lover threatened to end their relationship. He didn't want to live with someone who had children. The children interfered with their affair, or so he said. For this she was going to jail for thirty years. The reality of the two children dying in their car seats in the back of a car as it descended into the depths of a body of water was no less horrifying than the fact that their mother had been sleeping with her stepfather since she was fifteen. It was possible that the stepfather and the woman's mother (who knew that her husband and daughter were lovers) might go on trial as well, that these people were the real murderers. Then there was the father of the two children, who publicly stated that his wife should receive the death penalty, acknowledging his own murderous tendencies as well. Here he is at the trial with his new girlfriend. Under other circumstances, one might feel happy that he has a new lover of his own, that he was moving on in life, that he didn't care what anyone thought. That he had survived, after all, the death of his two children. But for some reason I can only feel contempt for everyone involved. I sometimes wonder, in fact, why laws exist at all, since most people seem to be following their own instincts anyway, no matter what. No penalties for anything you do. No jail sentences. If you do away with restrictions, you might end up creating an atmosphere where a new kind of love—a love that evolves out of freedom, not fear—is possible.

6

She was the type of woman who was probably used to deflecting the stares of men in public places: tall, with shoulder-length blonde hair, high cheekbones, a model's complacent beauty. There were some women (or so he imagined) who might be receptive to the approaches of a strange man, who didn't cringe from talking to a stranger on the subway, but he doubted that she was one of them. There were some women who might even welcome the company of a stranger, if only to pass the time; a transient encounter, a filler—meaningless, unthreatening. Not this one, he thought. He could only guess how this particular woman might respond if he actually spoke to her. Every situation is different; it all depends on who's speaking, right?

And why, in a million years, would anyone speak to me?

7

It was Hank, my former partner, who introduced us. A wedding party for a cop in the 9th Precinct whom we both knew way back when. Marrying a Russian woman, oddly enough. That was the connection, why Irina was there. She was a friend of the bride. At the moment we were introduced I didn't know she was living with someone else. Five minutes after we started dancing she said: "Do you want to sleep with me?" It was the first time a woman had asked me that question. Happily, I had the wit to respond by saying, "Some time." It made her laugh. By the end of the dance she had her hands on my ass. We weren't dancing as much as swaying. She was the first woman I'd ever met who didn't make me work to get her into bed. Couldn't understand how someone so beautiful would want to go to bed with me. You can have anyone you want, why me? I still had a vestige of pride—what pride was left after a marriage that ended after seventeen years—so I tried to act confident, like it was no big deal. Confidence is more attractive than insecurity. We were dancing to Marvin Gaye, the singer who was murdered in a motel room by his father. People made fun of Marvin Gaye because of his name. There was a rumor that he liked to dress up in women's clothing. People ridicule others out of jealousy, what other reason? We were dancing to "I Heard It Through The Grapevine," swaying in the center of the living room. Then "What's Going On?" came on and she took my hand and led me to a back bedroom, locked the door, and went down on me in the dark. If I was going to give that moment a caption, I'd say it was the start of my new life.

8

He used to lie on the beach at Santa Monica. That's how he spent his days. On a towel, propped on his elbows, staring at the ocean and the sky through dark glasses. It was a simple life; like Mersault, in *The Stranger*, he could take ultimate pleasure in sifting the sand through his fingers. The heat burning into the soles of his feet as he walked down to the water. It was a life that involved other people. You can connect with people by talking to them, by saying words that have meaning. And by writing: there was always that possibility, especially if no one was around, and he always carried a black sketchpad in his backpack, some magic markers, and a black felt-tip pen. He kept a kind of odd journal which consisted mostly of overheard conversations and things he read about in the newspaper. He didn't clip the articles from the paper, but he paraphrased them as if he were accumulating ideas for stories. Added to that were quotes from whatever books he was reading. His parents were overly educated types who had houses filled with books. After graduating high school, unlike most of his friends, he continued going to school, part-time, a class or two every semester, mostly at night. If nothing else, college was a good place to meet girls. So was the beach, for that matter. He lived in an apartment with two or three other guys, but mostly he slept over at the house of whatever woman he was seeing. Make that plural: there was always more than one woman at a time. He preferred women who were more interested in sex than falling in love, and that made it easier to be elusive without anyone getting hurt. He didn't want anyone to be hurt because he was being unfaithful. He didn't have relationships with women; he had sex with them, ate meals with them. Sometimes, after making love, the woman would prepare a meal. Sometimes they were content to lie in bed in silence, listening to music and smoking cigarettes. Sometimes they would make love two or three times. The women he liked most were the ones who talked about the books they were reading. Or movies. Whenever he met someone, the first thing he did was check out the books on their shelves. He was amazed that some people were proud of the fact that they didn't read anything. It just wasn't part of the repertoire of possible things to do for a lot of people. Books were associated with going to school. They were torture instruments that someone had invented. When the women he was with asked him what he did, he said he liked to read books. That was the test. It seemed important to have something in common with the person you spent time with. After sex and food there had to be something meaningful going on when you talked. His ideal woman was someone who had read books that he had never heard of before. The best relationships were those where you learned about what the other person knew.

He had a list of phone numbers. "Can I come over?" he would ask. It wasn't necessary to say anything else. If the woman was busy, no problem, he would try someone else. He would lie on the beach reading and listening to the radio. His parents were separated. His father lived in Los Angeles with his girlfriend, who was twenty years younger. His mother lived in a small town north of San Francisco, the town of his childhood. Every few months he hitchhiked north to see his mother, who lived with her boyfriend in a house overlooking the ocean. When he stayed there, he slept in a tent on the front lawn. He would sit on a ledge watching the night traffic over the Pacific—the airplanes bound for Japan, the shooting stars, the UFOs. He would read himself to sleep by flashlight like he did when he was a child.

9

They met in Bloomingdales. The two young women trying on hats, the man at the next counter. Eye contact. Lunch. His car was parked in an underground lot. He lived in Queens. It was a hundred degrees. A tape deck, sixties music. One woman up front, the other in back. A house with a driveway, air conditioning, and a thousand CDs alphabetized by title. The guy showed them his gun collection. Photos of his kids. Is that your first wife? One of the women dozes off while the guy takes the other one into the back bedroom. They undress in time to the music, The Supremes. Later, he takes a shower while the first woman watches TV. In the old days, he says, I used to have sex eight times a day. Now I'm lucky if I can do it twice.

10

All my therapists plied me with questions about my relationship to my parents. That was the heart of psychology, as far as I could tell: how you were affected by your parents. It was a universal dilemma. Everyone was affected by their parents in some way. You could not go through your life without being affected by your relationships to the people who brought you into the world. But how? What could I tell them? My therapy was a sham. I cheated my way through the hour by giving the therapist a glimpse of who I might be. The idea of going to a therapist and telling this person your life story, much less your secret thoughts and feelings, was too arbitrary. There had to be a reason for trusting this specific person other than the fact that he or she had a license to practice as a therapist. Most of the therapists I went to when I was in high school were men, except for one, a woman in her late fifties who spent the hour adjusting her skirt over her knees. She thought I was staring at her legs, and as a consequence all I wanted to do was talk to her about how I wasn't staring at her legs, that I wasn't interested in sleeping with her. I had the feeling, every time she adjusted her skirt over her knees, that she was drawing attention to her body. It was she who put the idea of sex into my mind. After a few weeks, it occurred to me that we might be better off having sex for an hour than sitting opposite one another and saying nothing, and though I wasn't particularly attracted to her, it was hard to think about anything else. I wondered if she was married. I asked her if she was married and she asked me why I was asking and I said "no reason" and she said that she had once been married when she was younger but it had only lasted a few months. It had been a mistake, and she had never married again. At the time, I wondered if that meant she had never slept with anyone since her marriage had ended. My next question, since she seemed to have no aversion to talking about herself, was whether she wanted to sleep with me, but I couldn't ask it. The way it entered my head was "Do you want to fuck?" and I had to smile to myself at the thought of saying such a thing.

11

He saw her out of the corner of his eye, just a movement in a landscape where everything else was motionless. Where it was too hot to do anything but wipe the sweat from your forehead and eyes. He was coming from lunch with his agent, Martha Block, at a restaurant near Union Square where he'd had too much to drink and eat, and he wanted to lie down for an hour or take a cold bath before resuming work on the book which his agent was encouraging him not to write. He would try to nap for awhile, then get to work by nightfall, when it was cooler.

The first name that came into his mind was Margaret, but it wasn't her.

He was about to climb the steps to the door of his building when she was in front of him, practically blocking his way. Flushed, wide amber eyes, her mouth open as if she were about to burst out laughing.

"I know you don't remember me," she began. "I was your student, five years ago."

"You were in the last class," he said.

"What do you mean?"

"That was the last class I ever taught."

"You were fired, I remember, everyone thought it was unfair."

"It was a blessing in disguise, really. What did you say your name was? I remember you, I remember your face, but I'm bad with names."

He wanted to say, right then, even before she told him his name: Do you want to come upstairs? In the old days, he wouldn't have hesitated.

"Yes, of course," he said, once she told him her name, just her first name, and he knew that she knew he didn't remember her.

"I read your book," she said.

He laughed. Everyone had read his book. It was a mystery to him why. Why anyone would bother reading the book or why he had bothered writing it. He had written it to prove to himself that he could do it but that didn't mean anyone else had to care. It would take the average reader four or five hours, and even that amount of time, the length of a plane trip from San Francisco to New York, seemed too long. "A good read," the critics had said, as if this was the highest praise imaginable. And now his agent and his publisher wanted him to write a fucking sequel. A series of books, really, using the same characters. Make it easy for your reader, Martha had said. They want something familiar.

And now this young woman, in her short skirt, her turquoise earrings, her bare arms, was going to tell him how much she "loved" his novel. It was the standard line. Possibly she had even been waiting for him outside his building, in the cafe across the street, waiting to tell him how much she had loved his book. And that she wanted to sleep with him as a kind of reward. That would happen too.

"I'm a writer," she said. "I write stories. Your class—you—inspired me. I started writing because of you."

"I don't believe it," he said, laughing again.

"But it's true. Why don't you believe it? You were a terrific teacher. All the books—all the books you ever mentioned in class—I read every one."

"I'm flattered," he said. And then: "Where do you live?"

She shrugged, gesturing with her hand, as if giving a direct answer to the question was too difficult. Or as if the answer was superfluous. Not appropriate. Why should he care where I live?

"You want me to read your stories? You want me to help you?"

She lowered her head.

"You're too busy. Why should you help me?"

"It's true, I'm busy. I'm trying to write another book."

"You should let me read it. We could trade manuscripts."

"I never let anyone read what I'm writing. Not even my agent. Not until it's done."

"I'm not 'anyone,'" Renee said.

Then he realized they were in a play and his next speech was supposed to be: "I'd like you to read my book. It's only about half-done, but I'm stuck. My agent hates it, hates the thought of it. She wants me to write another detective book. Maybe I'll do it some day, but not now. And I'd like to read your stories too. I mean it, though I don't know whether I can help you. The most I can do, if your stories are any good, is recommend you to my agent. Why don't you give me your phone number, I'll call you tonight, we'll make plans."

A Japanese woman in leather shorts walked by smoking a cigarette. A sanitation worker in the cab of his trunk honked at her as he drove by and she turned around and gave him the finger. A matronly woman with blue hair was walking her daschund with a newspaper under her arm and a plastic bag. Withered leaves cast lifeless shadows along the edge of the curb. Two guys in dreadlocks sat on the stoop of a discount record store, two buildings down from the apartment where he lived, smoking a joint. A policewoman swinging her nightstick was walking west up St. Marks Place from Tompkins Square Park. Disco music from a radio in the window of an upstairs apartment.

He was supposed to say—this was an earlier draft— "Do you want to come upstairs?" And she would say: "Let me get my things. I left my bag across the street." If it was inevitable that they go to bed together, why not now? In the old days, he would have made that assumption—with his students, with anyone—but that was then. Nothing was inevitable. He had no need to sleep with her, or anyone. The illusion that he had some control over what he did was better than having no control at all. But given this—here was this person in front of him, waiting for him to make a move—he didn't know whether becoming more civilized, taking nothing for granted, was a good thing. To simply say—"Give me your phone number, I'll call you"—sounded feeble, a misnomer, as if he was letting an opportunity pass.

"Give me your phone number," he said, "I'll call you."

"Tonight," she said, "tonight would be a good time."

"Then I'll call you tonight."

"And you'll show me your book?"

"Of course," he said. "I'll show you everything."

HARRY CRAY

The first thing he saw when he entered the apartment was the girl tied to the chair. There were five cops in uniform in the hallway behind him. Each of them had a gun and was pointing it into the entrance of the apartment. It was what they had learned during the grueling months of apprenticeship at The Police Academy, the proper procedure for entering an apartment where a killer was hiding.

The young woman in the chair had a strip of masking tape over her mouth. She wore a pale blue nightgown with tiny flowers embroidered along the sleeves. There was a white bow hanging down the front of the nightgown, but her shoulders and neck were bare. The light from the kitchen window behind her dovetailed across her back. It was like an aura, as if she were having a religious experience. There was a cloud of dust in the air around her head and her hair billowed over her shoulders and arms. Her hair was red and curly and very thick. There were droplets of sweat and tears on her high cheekbones. She was crying, but she couldn't wipe away her tears; they just welled up in the corner of her eyes and spilled out. Her nipples were erect against the fabric of the nightgown, as if someone had been kissing them. As if the danger was making her excited. It was her hair he noticed first, the reddish tint that seemed to hold the light coming in from the window, then the terror in her eyes. The way she suddenly tilted her head toward the door of the bedroom as if to say "He's there. The man you're looking for is in the bedroom with my friend."

Of course, when he kicked open the bedroom door, he hadn't expected to find Irene. Didn't know the woman's name or her relationship to the woman in the chair. He didn't know what to expect, really. The best equalizer in unpredictable situations is a weapon in your hand. Anything can happen when you confront a murderer in an enclosed setting. There's no way to predict what the person in the apartment will do.

Harry Cray stood in front of the door and said Eddie's name to himself; then he said it out loud.

He said, "Put your gun down, Eddie. We're coming in."

The five cops crouched behind him like lemurs, holding their guns with both hands. Harry thought, for a split second, of his daughter Veronica. Seventeen years old, a freshman in college. The girl in the chair was probably older than his daughter. There was no similarity between them, really, except that they both reminded Harry of something he couldn't have. Something he wanted that was always out of reach. There it was, like a brass ring, just beyond his grasp. There it was—a gift, an offering—but when he blinked it disappeared.

"It's over, Eddie," he said.

He couldn't believe the guy thought he could escape.

All the cops were in the room now and there was the woman, obviously dead, whom he was supporting with one arm while he pressed the gun against the side of her face. The last thing Harry wanted to do was kill Eddie Perez, but the guy was giving him no choice. It was just a matter of time, though. It was Eddie's decision whether he wanted to spend the rest of his life in jail or die in the moment.

The woman whom he was holding up as a hostage was naked. Her arms hung at her sides like a broken doll. Her head lolled back against Eddie's shoulder as if it was unhinged. There was blood on the bed sheets. Harry wanted to return to the kitchen and untie the woman in the chair. He felt like he was on a treadmill going backward, that there was no beginning or end, that he was on the edge of an invisible precipice, and that if he wasn't careful he would slip off into the dark. He wished that someone else had the wherewithal to pull the trigger. He had had this feeling before, that he was drifting out of his body, floating like a ghost in the corner of the ceiling. He pointed the gun at Eddie Perez. One of the cops behind him shouted "Do it, do it!" as if he couldn't understand why Harry Cray was waiting, or what he was waiting for.

The woman tied to the chair heard the gunshot and knew it was over. It was Harry, as he untied her hands, who told her that her friend was dead. She rushed into the bedroom and cradled Irene's head against her breasts. Eddie Perez was sprawled on his back a few feet away but she didn't seem to notice. There were people coming up the staircase, the police commissioner, newspaper reporters, photographers. She knelt on the floor with her friend in her arms, oblivious to the swirl of activity, and he tried to protect her from the photographers circling around her like parasites, shaking his head when the reporters asked him to tell them what had happened. Who were these women anyway? Russian immigrants? It would be on the front page of the tabloids, the dead girl from Russia, the story about the two friends who had emigrated from Russia.

It was later that she told him everything. How Eddie Perez had come in the window and tied her to the chair and took her friend into the bedroom. They were in his office at the precinct and she was talking into a tape recorder. Sitting in a chair near his desk, sipping from a styrofoam cup of weak coffee diluted with powdered milk, wincing every time she took a sip. Not crying, as he might have expected, but talking to him as if something like this had happened before. As if she had expected it to happen.

They began going out together once a week. Initially it was Marina who called him, though she wasn't certain if it was for any other reason than that he had told her she should call him, that he had given her his home number. It was there, on the back of the small card he had handed her when she left the precinct. There was not much she could do except tell the story of what had happened into a tape recorder. There was no reason for anyone to doubt that she was telling the truth.

Marina didn't tell Harry Cray about her boyfriend. She was planning to but wanted to put it off as long as possible. She didn't want Harry to think she went out with gangsters.

They met at cafés in the East Village, not far from where Irene had been murdered. Or restaurants, where he sometimes wore a tie. She tried to get him to talk about what was happening in his life. She asked him questions about his marriage. At first he wasn't sure what to say, what to include or leave out. He didn't understand why she was interested, why she wanted to see him. It was she who called him, who kept him on the phone telling him how she spent her days. They sat in a coffeehouse on Avenue A surrounded by strangers. People who spoke in foreign languages or in heavy accents. Everyone smoked and looked preoccupied.

He told her about a woman who had been murdered on East 10th Street, just a few blocks away. A woman named Yvonne de Marco who worked as a prostitute in a hotel near Times Square and who starred in porn movies. Yvonne de Marco was not her real name. Marina paid close attention to everything he said. He could see it in her eyes, that she was listening, that she would remember everything. The story about Yvonne de Marco was in the newspapers. All the cops at the precinct had heard of her. There were videos in her apartment with her name on the box. Harry Cray took one home with him but didn't watch it.

Harry Cray never went to college. It wasn't an option. His parents had never even graduated from high school. His only goal was to earn enough money so he could rent his own apartment. He found jobs through people he knew, through friends of friends, mostly in stores where time passed too slowly and he had to pretend he was someone he wasn't. He didn't want to spend his life smiling at strangers in the hope of seducing them into buying something. And he hated working for someone else. Someone suggested that he become a bartender. Someone else suggested he become a cop. Eventually he saved enough money so he could rent an apartment, so he could be free of the claustrophobia of family life, where every day was the same and where no one said anything. His parents barely talked to each other and slept in separate beds. His older sister was married and living in California. She had followed a similar path. She had graduated from high school and worked at a job she hated so she could save money and move out. Now she was living with her boyfriend in San Jose. She had a job during the day and went to school three nights a week. She encouraged Harry to go to college. She told him that he should move to California. The only thing they really had in common were their feelings about their parents. It was like death, like dying, inside that apartment.

It wasn't until he was with Sara that he actually began attending college, if only to catch up with her, going one night a week. Anthropology, psychology, history. He was looking for something that interested him. The question of why people acted the way they did seemed relevant to his life as a detective. This made sense and the police department actually paid for it. Harry felt inferior, like Sara knew more than he did because she had graduated college, because she could talk about things (books, authors, paintings, pieces of music) that he had never heard of. He couldn't understand why she might be interested in someone like him. When her friends came for dinner, he sat in silence, usually, listening but not listening, as if everyone was talking in a language he didn't understand, until someone asked him about his job: Any new cases? That's the word they used, "cases." Are you working on any new cases? Or, more flippantly: Did you kill anyone recently? The idea of eating dinner with a cop was a novelty to most people. Are you carrying a gun? Obviously, if you were a cop, there was a gun stashed in the apartment somewhere.

Once, when he went to meet Marina in the café on Avenue A, she was sitting at a table in the corner reading a book of Chekhov's stories. She said that she had read it many times before in Russian but she was reading it in English for the first time. She confessed that in recent months she had begun to think in English and that where before it had taken her fifteen minutes to read a page in English she was now able to read almost as proficiently as she could read in Russian. Harry took the book from her hands. There was a reproduction of a painting of a woman in a white hat on the cover. He said the name to himself, Anton Chekhov. He thumbed through the book as if he were familiar with the author's work, while in fact he had never heard of him.

"Which story are you reading?" he asked.

And she told him: "'Lady With Lapdog.' Do you know it?"

He returned the book to her, shaking his head, and hoped that she would change the subject, but instead she began telling him what the story was about. The main character was a forty-year-old man who falls in love with a woman he sees on the boardwalk in Yalta. He's married, both of them are married, and the man has had many affairs. After the woman's vacation is over, she returns to her husband in St. Petersburg, and eventually the man returns to his wife in Moscow. But he can't forget about her; he thinks that she's not like all his other girlfriends, women he slept with a few times and instantly forgot. He travels to St. Petersburg and stands outside the building where she lives with her husband but never sees her. Finally, he goes to the opening night of a concert, and of course she's there. They begin meeting again, this time in a hotel in Moscow. They have a secret life now, but they're in love with one another, they're really in love, and living out a lie feels tawdry and sad.

"That's it?" Harry said.

"The story isn't important," Marina answered. "I know it must sound stupid. But if you read it—I've read it a million times in Russian—you'll understand what I mean."

She looked at him as if she was the woman, Anna

Sergeyevna, and he was the man, Gurov, and that they were meeting together secretly like the characters in the story. But there was no reason to have any secrets, not from Harry Cray. You could tell him anything. The next day he bought the book, and when he was alone later that night he stretched out on his bed with the pillows propped against the wall and read the story.

Everyone told Harry Cray, when his marriage ended, that life would get interesting in a way he could never imagine until he was actually living it. He'd been married to the same woman for seventeen years and had never slept with anyone else. He had been twenty-two when they first met. Sara had been more experienced. She had had at least two serious relationships before she met Harry, and had slept with at least two dozen other men, or so she said, though most of them for only one night. She had told him all this before they were married, just in case it bothered him. If it bothered him maybe he wasn't the type of person she should marry. She told him that on more than one occasion she had slept with someone whose name she didn't know, and whom she never saw again, and that she had once slept with two guys at the same time. She told him about meeting a man on the subway and spending three days in his bed. Harry had pretended that what she was telling him didn't upset him, that he could handle it. He knew, instinctively, that she was testing him, and chose to believe that most of what she told him wasn't true, or that it was an exaggeration of the truth. When she said that she had slept with dozens of guys before him, maybe she only meant "a dozen," and had said "dozens" to see how he would react.

Harry could no longer remember the names of the women he had slept with before he met Sara. They were like blurred snapshots in the back of his mind that had faded beyond recognition. He remembered feelings of embarrassment and shame connected with a sense of pleasure that seemed to be happening to someone else. He remembered feelings of longing and desire that dissipated when the fantasy was translated into something real. Imagining touching a woman's body was different from actually doing it. Even with Sara, he had allowed himself to be seduced. It was she who had approached him, who put her hand on his arm in the middle of their first conversation, who had leaned towards him so he could see down the front of her blouse. He tried to stay focused on her eyes when they talked, but it was hard not to stare at her body when he thought she wasn't looking. He lit her cigarette and she touched his hand with her fingers as a way of thanking him. On the night he met Sara it had been over a year since he had slept with anyone. His few male friends thought he was crazy because he was so passive when he was around women. Some of his friends offered to set him up with sisters and cousins but he turned them down. He had walked Sara home from the bar where they had met, where she had gone, or so she told him later, with the specific intention of picking someone up, something she did frequently when she didn't have a steady boyfriend. "I just wanted to fuck someone," she said, testing him again. He had walked her home and she had asked him if he wanted to come upstairs. (Not for a drink. Not for anything. Wasn't it obvious what she wanted? Didn't he want the same thing?) She was living in a hole-in-the-wall on the fifth floor of a walk up on Avenue B, temping by day in a law office uptown, taking classes at NYU at night. Going to bars and picking up guys on weekends. Getting drunk. The guy she had been living with had moved out when he came home unexpectedly from work one afternoon and found her in bed with someone else. Harry would have been content with kissing her good night. Take her phone number and maybe call her in a week if he had the nerve. Even when they were alone together in her apartment he wasn't sure what she wanted. There was this blank space that had to be filled but he wasn't sure with what. There were words, there was music, but he didn't know where to begin.

And then there was the ultimate moment when they were in bed together and he told her he was a cop. It was the next morning and he woke up with her head resting on his stomach, the bed sheets tangled on the floor, and the cry of what sounded like an owl or a coyote from one of the adjacent rooftops. Sara (he didn't know her last name) was still asleep and he was frightened of waking her up if he moved too suddenly. He wasn't certain he wanted her to wake up at all. He preferred lying in bed with a person who was asleep than one who would impose meaningless conversation on him. It was later, after they had sex again, after she had initiated sex as she had done the night before by simply taking his hand and putting it between her legs, climbing on top of him when he was too exhausted to lift his head from the pillow, that she actually asked him how he earned a living and he told her. "I'm a cop," he said, there was no way he could lie about it. After a long silence she asked: "Are you carrying a gun?" And then, after he showed it to her: "I've never fucked a cop before." He could still hear her voice. That was the way she talked.

They had a child almost immediately and then there had been complications with the birth that made it impossible for Sara to get pregnant again, and after that their sex life faded as well. She lost interest in sex for long periods of time and there was nothing Harry could do to make things better. Whatever he tried to do only made things worse. His job, certainly, didn't help, but Sara had known this before they were married. She had known that being a cop involved working odd hours, often the whole night, and that sometimes he had to change the direction of his life at the last minute (cancel plans they had made long in advance) to accommodate the demands of his job. It was hard to make plans in advance since who knew what might come up. And his job always took precedent over everything else, including time spent with his wife and daughter. That's what it meant to be a cop.

Sara had understood all this. She had pretended to

understand with the hope that things would change or that she would adjust to the exigencies of her husband's job, but it never happened the way she imagined. As long as the rest of their life was working, she would make the necessary adjustments to his schedule, his non-schedule, since every day was different, a function of random events. But if you asked her whether she was content with her role as the wife of a cop she would have said no without hesitation, or "I don't know what contentment means." She had listened to him patiently—for years—while he worried over his work. She would sit up all night with him when he couldn't sleep because he was worried about his job. He brought his job home with him, how could he do otherwise? There were no boundaries between his life as a detective and his roles as father and husband.

And then one day she stopped listening.

"I'm like a single mother," she told him, while they were still living together, "and I hate it."

They would go out on dates, to restaurants, once a week. Usually on his day off. Then he would put her in a cab and give her some money to pay the driver. At first she tried to refuse the money: she had a job, after all, and she didn't want him to think she was helpless, dependent on him, wanted him to erase the image he had of her tied to the chair. She was the only person he saw outside of work and the only woman he talked to other than his daughter, who was away at school. He and Veronica spoke on the phone, usually once a week, and every few weeks he sent her money.

He sat on the sofa in his studio apartment reading the book by Chekhov. It had been a new experience, entering a bookstore with the intention of buying a specific book, and then asking the saleswoman where he could find it, the book of stories which Marina had been reading, the story about the woman and the dog. He had the book now, it made him feel closer to her. The next time they had dinner together they would have something to talk about. He wanted to know more about the reality of the words on the page and how they related to the rest of experience. He had always assumed that there was separateness between what happened in books and what you did with the rest of your life, that there was no relationship between the two. There was no logical reason why anyone should be interested in a reality that someone else invented. The only thing Harry ever read was the newspaper; at least that seemed to connect with a kind of reality that was familiar to him. The newspaper was like a book of separate stories which continued day after day. Each story had its own plot and characters. The story about the dead porn star had been on the front page of *The Daily News*. There was her photograph and her biography listing the names of all her movies. Harry was shocked that so many people had heard of her. Her real name, as it turned out, was Barbara Mahony. A runaway from the suburbs of Boston. He had contacted her parents and they had come to the city to claim their daughter's body. The day after she appeared on the front page of the newspaper there was no reference to her murder. It was only after they found the murderer that the newspaper would run the story again.

He was reading the story by Chekhov called "Misfortune" when the phone rang. He assumed it was someone from the precinct, that one of the people they were questioning had confessed. It was three in the afternoon, the end of September, and he had been thinking that what he'd like to do was take a drive in the country. In a few weeks the leaves would begin to change color. He could hear Sara's voice. It had been in his head all the time he was reading. He couldn't read a few lines without hearing her say something. The problem with reading was it took too much work to keep interested. There was no way you could go off in your head and still be engaged in the book. As soon as he began thinking of taking a drive, he began imagining himself with Sara and Veronica. It was Sunday afternoon and they were riding through the country as if nothing had ever happened.

The apartment where Harry Cray lived was a few blocks north of 14th Street. In walking distance from the apartment where he used to live with Sara. It was the first apartment he saw when he moved out and he regretted not taking more time looking for a larger place. He had been seduced by the real estate agent, a young woman named Elaine. Almost immediately they were on a first-name basis. It shocked him whenever she called him Harry. She had seduced him with false intimacy and he had taken the apartment to please her. She had given him the impression that she would do anything he wanted. She leaned back against the kitchen sink and watched him as he toured the apartment. There was not much to see. Of course, he was thinking, I want to touch her but I can't. It wasn't permitted. They were alone in the recently painted unfurnished studio apartment. He never knew what a woman was feeling at any given time. The worst scenario was if he reached out and she pushed him away or screamed for help. He was a cop, after all. He would probably be suspended or fired. What he wanted was for her to make the first move, to give him permission. They were standing at the window staring out over 3rd Avenue. He could feel the sleeve of her blouse brushing against his arm. Then she moved toward him to point out something in the distance and he could feel her breast against the tip of his elbow. She seemed to be purposely letting him touch her in this way without acknowledging that it was happening. It took months, as a consequence, to get her out of his mind. It was hard to be in the apartment without imagining her there. But now that he no longer thought about her he regretted ever taking the apartment. He didn't like eating and sleeping in the same room. He didn't plan to live alone forever, and there was no way that two people could share one room.

He was wearing a white long-sleeved shirt, unbuttoned. His feet were bare, propped up on a wooden trunk with the ankles crossed.

He had started out lying on the couch but began to

lose concentration. He would reach the right-hand margin and lose his way back to the next line. He knew that the only reason he was reading the book was because of Marina. To impress her. To prove to her that they might be interested in the same thing. Sometimes he felt he had nothing to talk about except his job and his daughter.

The Chekhov story was simple enough, and there was enough description so that he could visualize the characters, but his mind kept wandering, one thought dissolving into another, until he was no longer aware of himself in the present. All his thoughts always collapsed around the feeling of loss he had experienced when he and Sara broke up. The memory of her was like a virus inhabiting his body. It had been more than a year now.

It was Marina on the phone asking him if he wanted to have dinner. She knew it was short notice—why don't you come over in a few hours? She said it in a way that made him feel she would be hurt if he refused. His first instinct had been to say no, to go against what he really wanted.

In the past they had always met in restaurants or cafés in Manhattan, near her old apartment. She had promised to invite him over as soon as she settled in to her new place in Brighton Beach. It had been two months since the incident with Eddie Perez. The Russian community in Brighton Beach had been helpful in finding her an apartment. She was a kind of celebrity: there was a picture, along with one of Irene, in the newspapers. There was the story about the murder in the newspapers. A picture of Eddie Perez as well. Marina had assumed that Boris, Ivan's boss, was responsible for any unexpected good fortune. All he had to do was call a real estate broker or a landlord and tell them to give her whatever apartment she wanted. For once she was grateful to him. There was no way she could have continued living in the apartment where Irene was murdered. Ivan was still in jail. He would be out in two months. And then what? Just the day before she had taken the train to the prison upstate. It was a tedious ride, four hours each way, just for a half hour visit. Ivan looked older and kept mopping his face with a dirty handkerchief. He had lost about twenty pounds. His hair was thinning, his chin covered with a layer of stubble. He kept blinking, several times in succession, as if he was staring into the sun, and never once looked at her directly. She couldn't imagine ever going to bed with him again.

They were sitting on the sofa in the living room area of her apartment and she was showing him photographs from Russia. They were drinking wine. There was Irene, the woman who was killed. There was Marina and Irene, as teenagers in Odessa, with their arms around each other. Harry could feel the pressure of her thigh against his as she leaned forward to turn the pages of the album. She told him about the baby who had died, Irene's baby, about her secret lover, but she didn't talk about herself, what her own life was like in Russia. She was wearing jeans and a black woolen jersey. He was aware that their bodies were touching but he wasn't sure that it meant anything to her, that it was a signal. It was the first time they had ever been alone together in an enclosed space, a room. He felt a kind of equanimity when he was with her, a feeling that he didn't want to end. He was frightened that if he tried to make love to her and she didn't want to, it would ruin their friendship.

This was her world, anyway, the place she came home to every day. He had been in her other apartment as well, the one that she shared with Irene. She was telling him about Irene. Then she stopped in mid-sentence and leaned her head back against the sofa. The apartment had been empty when she moved in. One day a moving van arrived with new furniture. No one had even called her to ask her what she needed. A sofa, a dining room table, a set of chairs. No doubt Boris was behind it all, who else? Marina had stood at the apartment door dumbfounded as the movers unloaded the furniture and carried it up the stairs. All she had to do was sign her name on a piece of paper and the furniture was hers. Ivan's and hers.

She took Harry's hand and brought it to her lips. She took each of his fingers and put them in her mouth, one at a time. Sucking on them, slowly, deliberately—no one had ever done this to him before. He watched her as if the hand belonged to someone else, watched her unfolding in front of him, her eyes closed. Her neck muscles bulged slightly, tightening, as if pieces of rope had caught beneath her skin. He moved his free hand along her body as her legs parted. He began fumbling with her belt and the buttons of her pants.

He wonders about all her other lovers. Here or in Russia, what she wants him to do. What's permitted. She puts her hand on top of his head and rests her legs on his shoulders as he moves his fingers inside her. He wishes she had worn a skirt so they could make love with their clothing on. All he would have to do, then, is lift her skirt and come inside her. This way is too clumsy. They're wearing too much clothing. He doesn't want to stand up and unbuckle his pants, but when he does she leans forward and takes his cock in her mouth, sucking on it the way she did with his fingers. Generously, with expertise, using her hand and her tongue simultaneously. It scares him for a moment, how good she is, as if she had it all planned, that she would invite him over and that this would happen. Obviously it's something she wants to happen.

There are people talking in Russian in the hallway. An argument, a man and woman fighting. He can tell by their tones. The rush of footsteps and then a siren in the street. Marina moves her mouth away for a moment and says the word "air." She continues to hold his cock, rubbing it gently, flicking at the tip with her tongue. He wants to say now, "I want to come inside you," but he can't help himself. There's no now, no language for now, how do you say it in Russian? A Russian movie, the white tundra, everyone moving in slow motion.

In her bedroom now, she sits on a chair and he kneels in front of her. By the time she comes he has an erection again. He's excited without her touching him. No one touched him this way for years. Someone bending, someone kneeling, someone falling forward. They should rest for awhile and drink some more wine but he doesn't want to stop. Her body ripples beneath him as if she were swimming over the sheets. He's inside her now and it's calm, it's like evening. Like seeing the world through blue curtains. He leans down to kiss her nipple and she says "Harder." He's fucking her and biting her nipple at the same time. The idea that she might want him to hurt her excites him. It's not something he ever imagined doing to anyone. For years the only sex with Sara took place with the lights out when they were both exhausted. For years—he didn't know this—she had slept with other men when he was gone. A string of boyfriends, it was her whole world. While their daughter was at school she would spend whole days in her lovers' apartments. Harry Cray didn't have a clue. The last thing she wanted when they got into bed at night was to have sex with him.

She has a birthmark on the side of her neck, a purplish island of skin. The room contains a bed and an old mahogany dresser that the people living here before her had left in the apartment. There are photographs in frames everywhere, people out of her past. A wooden jewelry box on top of the dresser. She's not a particularly orderly person, but she cleaned up before he came. Stuffed the clothing in drawers and closets. She knew that this was going to happen. It was something inevitable, like a volcano that would someday explode. What she didn't know was whether it would ever happen again.

Harry Cray wanted to know about her other lovers. It was part of his mind-set, to discover clues to why someone acted the way they did. It would ruin everything if he thought too hard about why something was happening. To say that it was simply a gift was too easy. There was no paradigm—nothing that had happened in his past—to prepare him for this moment. He knew that this was what he wanted, ever since the moment when he saw her tied to the chair. In the street a car backfiring sounds like a gunshot and he remembers the way he pointed his gun at Eddie Perez while the other cops crouched behind him with their guns drawn, waiting for him to make a move. It seemed like all that had happened years ago, and to another person.

He pulled at her hair. There was some rust in it that he never noticed before and one long gray strand. She was kneeling on the bed in front of him and he grabbed her hair and pulled it. "Harder," she said. Again, it wasn't something he had ever imagined doing. It wasn't part of his fantasy world. He did it because he sensed that she wanted him to do it, that it gave her pleasure. It was like being with a prostitute, that's how it felt. What other people had told him, that you could do what you wanted if you paid for it. She didn't seem to care what he thought. All she wanted to do was give him pleasure. He had saved her life, so to speak. She knew that it was possible to fall in love, that anything was possible. Who had seen him come to her apartment? Was anyone spying on her? She knew that Boris kept tabs on her life, or she assumed he did. That was part of his job, that's why he was known as "The King of Brighton Beach." His loyalty was to Ivan. As far as he was concerned, she was just Ivan's whore.

It wasn't what he anticipated when she asked him to dinner. There had been no sign, up to that point, that she was interested in sleeping with him. The days of meeting at cafés and restaurants receded into the past. For now, and for the future, this was what they would do together, night after night. It seemed inevitable, in Harry's mind, that they would end up living together. She was coming, she was breathing heavily, she was raking her nails across his back. He was biting her nipples and moving his fingers inside her at the same time. Then she was on her back and he was on top of her with her legs resting on his shoulders. She was balancing her legs with her hands, raising them toward her as far as they could go, so he could penetrate her more deeply, as if the whole point of sex was to disappear into the body of the other person, a pillow behind her head to prevent it from hitting the wall.

It had been a long time since he had given anyone pleasure. It occurred to him that possibly she was faking it to make him feel better. How many orgasms can you have anyway? Once he was confused and wanted to ask her whether she had come, but he didn't. It seemed like she was breathing heavily, they were lying side by side and he was fucking her from behind. He found a position where they could fuck and he could touch her at the same time, so it was possible they might come simultaneously but it would probably take forever. She was lying on her back humming a song, a Russian folk song which her mother had taught her.

He hadn't smoked in years. She said, "Do you want one?" He took one of hers. He inhaled and didn't cough. He didn't know what time it was and he didn't know whether he was hungry. It was understood that they were just taking a break and he didn't have to leave. He could sleep over, they could make love all night if he wanted. He was amazed how different she looked, how her face had changed. The woman tied to the chair had vanished but this new person was a mystery. He wondered if there was a photo of her boyfriend on the top of her dresser with the other photos of Irene and her parents. He remembered asking her about how she found an apartment so easily and she had said that relatives had helped her. As a cop, he must know about all the Russian gangsters. There was probably a thick file on Boris. He felt sore but he didn't want to stop. They were in the shower and she was on her knees in front of him while the water sprayed in her face. She took his cock in her mouth, then stood up and turned around and practically touched her toes so he could enter from behind. She wanted him to slap her back but was frightened of asking. She didn't want to do anything that would scare him away.

He had told her about his life with Sara. The very first time that they had coffee together after Irene was murdered she had asked him if he had been married.

And what happened? She wanted to know why they had broken up after seventeen years. A long time, maybe too long, for two people to co-exist. He told Marina that he had underestimated his wife's needs. That he had assumed she was satisfied with their life together. Sometimes a week or two went by and they didn't have sex, but it didn't seem like anything was wrong especially when Veronica was still young. If he wanted to make love and she didn't, she would tell him she was exhausted and he realized that he was equally exhausted but had suggested making love because he thought that she wanted to, that she would connect not wanting to with a lack of interest. It went on for years that way. He didn't know whether it was true of all couples, that they gradually lost interest in one another sexually. The last thing he imagined was that she was sleeping with someone else, with other men, that it was happening all the time.

After the shower he dried her shoulders and arms with a towel. He dried her back. They stood in front of the bathroom mirror and he kissed her on the side of her neck. It was hard to juxtapose one thought with another, one body with another. They were looking into a prism, the mesh of colors. A hologram of bodies dissolving over liquid surfaces. "Dry my hair," she said and he began to rub her scalp with the towel. When he was finished she leaned over the bathroom sink and put him inside her.

They would get a mirror near the bed so they could watch themselves fucking. It was Sunday night and she had to get up the next morning and go to work. With

Harry it was different. He was always working, always on call. There was a message from Ricardo, his partner, on his beeper, with news that a woman had been murdered in her apartment on the Lower East Side, not far from where Marina used to live. He had told Ricardo that he would be there in an hour and more than that had passed. She said, leaning over the sink: "I want you to come one more time."

I wasn't friends with Yvonne de Marco, but we used to have coffee in her apartment. Maybe once every two weeks we would meet on the staircase or in the vestibule near the mailboxes. "Judith," she would say, spreading her fingers over the sleeve of my jacket, "let's have some coffee."

It was during the time when I was teaching English at the private high school in Brooklyn Heights. The time when I was involved with the Russians.

The cop was here for a second interview. Looked like he was tired of being a cop. I had seen the look on the faces of the men in my family. He and his partner had been here the night before. Now what did he want, more questions, the same questions? It seemed like it was more like a social call. I had sensed it the night before, a kind of longing in his eyes, like he wanted something I had and wasn't sure what it was. Love, sex—this is what everyone wants—but something more. Some mixture of the two. The anonymity of it all—that was my pleasure, making love to someone I didn't know. That's why Yvonne de Marco liked me. We could talk about men in a way that made sense to both of us. "You'd make a good whore," she once told me, and I knew what she meant.

It was the time when I would go to parties with Marina. Her boyfriend Ivan was in jail. This was before her friend came from Russia. Before the murder. Irene hadn't arrived yet—that would all happen later. I would shock Marina by going into bedrooms with two or three guys at the same time. Often I was the only non-Russian at the party. I had picked up a few words on my own—*Da pazhalsta, Spaseeba, harasho*—and began taking lessons with a retired Russian professor on the Upper West Side. Marina would laugh at my accent. We would have lunch together on the promenade in Brooklyn Heights.

The cop had told me his name the night before but I had forgotten it. Harry Cray, he said again. I offered him coffee. I always have a pot of coffee heating when I'm working. He sat at the kitchen table and I showed him my watercolors and collages and photographs. The wall was covered with them. I knew if he made a move I'd let him do anything.

He wanted to know about Yvonne. They had found her journals and were trying to figure out what her life was like. Did I remember anything specifically? I looked at him oddly. He had a pad on the table and a pen in his hand. There was something wrong with this picture. It was like some still in an old black-and-white B-movie from the fifties. Except that the detective wasn't wearing a hat or tie, like they did then.

He had a scar on his right cheek and I wanted to ask him: where, when? I wanted to touch it with my fingers.

I wondered if he had other scars: back, shoulder, thigh.

I told him a story:

We were having coffee, me and Yvonne. It must have been a month ago. She was really beautiful, thin and blonde, with these small perfect breasts. That's what she was famous for, really—it was a totally different look from the other porn stars. You could see how guys would get turned on. Have you seen her movies? There's always a scene with two guys, one on either side, each of them sucking on one of her breasts.

She once gave me a tape and I played about half of it. Porn isn't my thing, really. I like real life. I don't have much of a fantasy life. Anyway, we were talking in her living room and she was showing me photographs from her childhood, when she was a teenager growing up in Maine. You must know all this by now. You must know where's she from. Her real name. Anyway, finally I said straight out: How did it all begin? What happened?

And she knew what I meant but she wasn't going to tell me. She shook her head: Are you a shrink? Do you really care?

It was the beginning of my time with the Russians. I'd moved to New York after my marriage ended. We'd been living in San Francisco and it felt unhealthy being in the same town together. Just knowing the neighborhood and the building where he lived was a source of unhappiness, and I had to go out of my way to avoid places where we might meet. It was all too much trouble. One of us had to leave and since he had the job it was up to me to make a move. I mean, I had jobs too but it was easier for me to adapt. Or so he argued. And he didn't seem to care one way or the other whether we lived in the same city or not. He had a new girlfriend by then. While I just had a lot of different guys who liked me because I liked to fuck.

She was wearing a white t-shirt, her breasts were pointing out at me.

I wanted something, a story. We smoked and drank coffee.

And you? she kept saying. She didn't want to talk about herself.

Of course I knew the answer. Someone was offering her money. She was in high school when she met some guy in a bar, he was from Boston, and he lured the innocent country girl into the big city. Only she wasn't that innocent. I already had a reputation, she said. I just wanted guys to like me. It was the only thing that was important. I would have guys come back to the house after school.

So this guy got me a job in an escort service. That's what it was called. He was my pimp, in a way. We lived together, me and some other woman. He slept with us on alternate nights, though some nights he didn't even bother coming home. Being someone's escort was more interesting than having sex with someone in a hotel room, though often being an escort ended up back in someone's hotel and it was understood as part of the deal that she would do whatever the guy wanted. Once, she told me, she was at a party where she was the only woman. It was part of the arrangement that she would have sex with everyone at the party. She had just turned eighteen. Most of the men at the party were in their fifties. Most of them probably had daughters who were older than she was. Probably some of these men thought they were making love to their daughters. Most of them, as it turned out, were too drunk to get an erection. It made them angry at her. The only way they could get excited was to slap her around. They began to argue among themselves, some of them feeling protective of her while the others wanted to leave scars, carve their initials on her stomach. One of them had a gun and happily he was one of the men who was trying to protect her. Things had gotten out of control. The guy with the gun told Yvonne to get dressed. He said: "I'll get you out of here." Yvonne was grateful but she didn't trust anyone at this point, especially not someone who liked to point his gun in people's faces. As soon as she reached the street she began running.

You're not writing any of this down, are you? I said to Harry Cray. You didn't come here to talk about the murder.

It's odd to be as intimate as my husband and I were—

sleeping together every night for eight years—and then not to be. The opposite of intimacy—of sharing everything with someone else—is distance. I felt my heart had split into a million tiny fragments. Shards of someone no one cared about anymore. Broken—that's what it means—split in two. Shattered. There are all these words you can use to describe this feeling, but words don't do it justice. There's always something beyond the words that can't be defined.

I met Marina at the school where I worked in Brooklyn Heights. We ate lunch together on the promenade overlooking the river, with the Statue of Liberty in the distance. Occasionally a convoy of helicopters carrying some famous dignitaries would descend from behind a bank of dark clouds. We unwrapped our sandwiches and drank coffee from a thermos. This was before Irene, Marina's girlfriend, arrived here from Russia, before Eddie Perez climbed through the window. It was during a time when Marina's boyfriend Ivan was in jail. We sat on a bench looking out over the river. We drank coffee and shared a cigarette. Marina wore a subtle, almost invisible shade of lipstick, and she left a stain on the filter which I breathed in along with the smoke. It was easy to feel that one could fall in love with her. I told her about my marriage and the bad ending in the hope that talking openly would bring us closer. I told her that I felt like I was recovering from some illness that no one had ever heard about before and for which there was no cure.

"There is a cure," she said. "You have to fall in love

again."

I wanted to tell her that I was love with *her,* but I couldn't say it.

She began inviting me to parties where I was the only non-Russian. According to Marina, most of the Russian men she knew were intimidated by American women. I tried to make it easy for them, like a goodwill ambassador; whether they could speak perfect English wasn't important, I reassured them, as they recounted the stories of all the American women who had snubbed them because their accents were all wrong and how I was different. I was always surrounded by many men, I could take my pick, and occasionally I went home with someone without even knowing his name. In those days, Russian names sounded interchangeable to me. Marina would call me up the day after a party and tell me about all the men who had called her asking for my phone number. I had the feeling that all the Russian women who came to these parties hated me. Not only was I some kind of foreign specimen—exotic, really, a hothouse flower under glass—in the eyes of their men, but I wasn't interested in playing games. Most women, or so I've heard from the men I've been with, like to tease you before they sleep with you, if they sleep with you at all. They like to make you think they're interested in sleeping with you and then they turn you down. All the Russian women at the parties hated me. They knew that what I could offer their men was as persuasive as a shot of heroin. They could see it in the way I danced with their men. They could hear the siren's song when they saw me coming. They could hear the sound of the boat crashing into the rocks.

Perversely, I began going out with a guy named Dimitri who was married and had three kids.

The idea was that he would tutor me in Russian and I would teach him English, but of course that didn't happen.

We saw each other secretly. The only night we ever spent together was the first night we met. His wife Natasha was out of town with the kids. After that, things became complicated. He told his wife that he was taking English lessons at a school on 34th Street. He enrolled at the school, bought the book, but instead of attending classes he came to see me. The only person I told was Marina, who shook her head in disbelief (of all the guys, why had I chosen the one who was married?) and warned me about Dimitri's wife. Natasha was the sister of a guy named Boris who was apparently a big deal in the Russian community.

Meaning what?

"He's a fucking gangster," Marina said. "He kills people."

At night, before going to bed, I imagined having sex with Marina. This was my real secret, of course, what I couldn't tell anyone. I had never been with a woman before—a few drunken kisses with my college roommate—but I wasn't frightened. I'd been hurt by my former husband and I felt I was going to get hurt again with Dimitri. There was no way he was ever going to leave his wife and be with me, so why bother? The question of what was important was on my mind a lot. Did anything matter? I imagined touching Marina's breasts, that was all. That was important, the sense of permission, what she would do if I acted on my feelings. If she would let me if I asked. I imagined a scenario where I said "I want to sleep with you" and she said "Yes, I know." The relationship between my feelings and desires was like the horizon line between ocean and sky, with different shades of blue on either side.

It's hard to know what other people are thinking, what they want. My relationship with my husband had been founded on the desire to give pleasure. During the first few months we spent as much time as possible in bed. I would go to his apartment and within minutes we were having sex. That was before we began living together. The perfect relationship is when each person is thinking about the other's pleasure at the same time. The normal state is one of imbalance, where one person loves and desires the other person more. For this person, the relationship is more important than his or her own self. At least in the beginning there's some chance that things can be mutual. The fact that you know everything's going to change eventually—that the balance is never static—is reason enough to work at sustaining the initial rush of desire. It's like keeping a flame alive, if only because the alternative—desirelessness, lack of love—is too horrible to contemplate. A glimpse of the void, the abyss of absence.

I asked Dimitri about Boris, Natasha's brother. What would happen if she found out? Was there any chance of her finding out? Marina told me that Natasha was suspicious by nature (though the community of Russian immigrants was burgeoning, everyone still knew everyone else's business) and he wouldn't put it past her to check up on her husband. When I asked Dimitri about his wife's brother he pretended that he couldn't understand. He raised his eyebrows and shrugged. He sat at the kitchen table rolling a cigarette and I felt like punching him in the face for not being straight with me.

"Boris," I repeated. "Isn't that his name?"

It was time to go. The way to avoid responsibility was to walk out the door. He made a sweeping gesture as if to ward off a swarm of bees. The whole world was conspiring against him. He had thought that coming to this country would make a difference, but it was worse. Capitalism was worse than communism. Everything he had been brought up to believe about capitalism was true. People would stab their own mothers to get an advantage over someone else. According to Dimitri, people here had even less sense of what it felt like to be free than they did in Russia. I knew that he could go on like this for hours, if I let him and if we had the time.

I had the feeling that I might not see him again, that this time something would really happen. I put my hand on his shoulder as a way of quieting him, and he reached out and touched my breast. He lifted my striped jersey and covered my nipple with his mouth. His need for sex (sex as a form of comfort) was greater than mine; it was what attracted me most. And I liked making love with clothing on, his pants around his ankles as I straddled him in one of the uncomfortable wooden chairs which I'd bought at the Salvation Army.

He felt guilty, or so he said, because all we ever did was go to bed together; then he would leave. We had been lovers for two months and already I felt dragged down by the tentativeness with which we said goodbye. I could feel his semen dripping down my leg as we stood in the doorway. Marina's words echoed as if across a distant canyon and I pretended not to hear. We both knew that something might happen to prevent us from ever seeing each other again. And it was true—anything could happen. Not only was the relationship a dead end, but it was dangerous as well.

He was standing outside the building. His back was to me as I came up the street but I recognized him immediately. I was coming home from work with a plastic bag filled with groceries and some cans of cat food. My shoulder bag was heavy and I wanted to sit down. It was the moment of the day that I felt most tired. On days when I had time I took a brief nap when I returned home from work. It was the moment of every day that I hated living alone. What would be nice was if someone was there when I came from work to massage my neck and back. Sometimes when I returned home from work I took a bath and fell asleep in the tub with the water lapping around my shoulders.

He was staring at the windows of Yvonne de Marco's apartment. Or possibly he was staring at mine? Whatever, the fact that someone had been murdered in the building gave him a reason to be there.

It was when we were lying in bed together, an hour later, that he asked me where I was coming from and I said I was coming from work, from my job. That's where I was coming from when I saw him outside the building. Is that what he meant, "coming from"? For a moment I wasn't sure. I had become accustomed to translating everything Dimitri said into some reasonable semblance of what he meant, but at least half the time I heard the opposite and said something inappropriate in response. But the cop's question was a simple one. It caught me off guard, as if he was setting a trap of some kind. I wondered if I was a suspect in Yvonne de Marco's murder or whether he thought that I knew something I wasn't telling him.

Finally I understood. He wanted to know where I worked.

It was the way he responded when I told him that changed everything. There's a reason why things happen the way they do. We were lying in my bed, under a sheet, his hand resting on my thigh. I wanted him to make me come but I knew it was too much to ask. It would happen—maybe—if we ever slept together again. And that was doubtful. I was already worried that he'd be in front of the building every day when I came home. I took his hand and placed it between my legs. It was at that moment he asked me, apropos nothing, where I was coming from when we met, and I told him the name of the school where I worked and what I taught.

"Marina," he said. He didn't say "Do you know Marina Tabachnikov?" He didn't phrase it in the form of a question. He simply sat up in bed and said her name.

Sleeping with the cop was a way out of my relationship with Dimitri. It was the first step. I had trouble ending relationships even when I knew they were going nowhere. Neither Dimitri nor the cop were particularly interested in pleasing me or concerned whether I thought of them as adequate lovers. Dimitri didn't have time. The whole idea of being unfaithful to his wife was unnerving to him; just the thought depleted him of whatever energy he needed to think of anyone's pleasure but his own. As much as he wanted to think otherwise, sleeping with me wasn't something he could do casually. And I wasn't easy, whether he had time or not; I had odd quirks which neither of these guys would understand in a million years. The reason I got married was because my husband was just like me, at least as far as sex was concerned. When I asked him to do something—something I wanted—he was more than happy to try to please me.

What I wanted was the guy to put his hands around my neck and try to strangle me. To pretend to strangle me. This involved trust and intuition. You had to pass the point where it seemed like you were acting. When I said "Stop," you had to continue. My husband couldn't believe it. You could say that was the main reason why we got married. It gave us the illusion that we shared everything, that the dreamlike moment when he knitted his fingers around my neck was enough to get us through any of life's difficulties. In comparison, all other issues seemed petty. This was the only reality. We could get up every morning and go to the same job every day of our lives, but none of it was real. Not in comparison to this.

And now I knew about him as well. Marina had told me about the cop who had saved her life. How she had wanted to do something in return but that she couldn't tell whether he wanted to sleep with her. I had been jealous, of course; it made me want to do something for her, so that she would want to please me, as well. The idea of translating gratitude into sex was an interesting concept. It seemed as good a reason to sleep with someone as any other. Someone saves your life—it's the least you can do.

He calls Sara to find out when Veronica is visiting and a guy answers, her new boyfriend.

"It's for you, babe," he hears him say.

And then Sara says—Harry imagines them in bed together—"Who is this?" As if the call interrupted something important. She sounds annoyed.

"It's only ten o'clock," Harry says. "It's not that late."

He can picture the bed, a shadow of himself lying where this guy's lying, the tensor light on the bedside table, his clothes folded over the back of a chair. The last time he saw her she'd been with another guy—they'd all met by accident outside the post office on 14th Street. A blonde guy with a silver earring who was half her age, at least. Sara didn't introduce him to Harry, who extended his hand anyway and touched the guy's arm as a form of acknowledgement. He had heard from Veronica that Sara had broken up with the blonde boyfriend and was seeing someone new. There wasn't much time lag between boyfriends and often they overlapped, so for a few weeks she was seeing two guys at once, on alternate nights, until she made a choice.

The reality of Sara's life is what Harry tries not to imagine. If he was making a movie this is what it would be like. The voice-over—himself talking—*We used to be married*. Then a close-up of Sara's face, sitting alone at a bar.

He would cast his life as a movie from the fifties, with Victor Mature playing the cop whose wife cheats on him.

There was a possibility of getting Rhonda Fleming for the role of Sara, but she was too beautiful.

Harry says: "I haven't heard from Ronnie in awhile. Just wondering when she was coming to town."

"Why don't you call her," Sara says.

"I do. I did, left a message, a couple of times, but she never calls back."

"I'm not surprised."

He wants to defend himself as a father. It's Sara's theory that his absences during Veronica's childhood have messed her up in ways they didn't even know about yet. And the fact that when people ask her about her parents she has to say: "My father's a cop."

What Sara never told Harry was about Veronica's boyfriend, a bicycle messenger named Flick who had dropped out of high school and whom she'd met in a bar on Ludlow Street. Whenever Veronica was in town Flick slept over. They would stay up most of the night listening to music and sleep most of the day. And on occasional weekends he would take the bus to visit her at school.

"Daddy thinks I'm still a virgin," Ronnie would say.

It was fun when she was in town and they both had boyfriends sleeping over. Mother and daughter, not a picture for Harry's eyes. He didn't know whether his daughter was a virgin or not. They never talked about sex. In high school she would mention some guy, going out on a date, that was normal, it would be unusual if she never went on a date, so she always told him. But since she was away at school there was no mention of any guys and Harry thought: That's good, she's doing her work.

Neither Sara or Harry know how little work she's

really doing.

"I don't think she's coming in this weekend," Sara says, though Ronnie often calls her at the last moment to say that she and Flick will be sleeping over. Sara has the feeling that Flick is taking money out of her wallet but she isn't sure.

She had met her new boyfriend on a train from Boston. They had ended up sharing a cab back to her place. He was the same age as Flick, just out of college. They'd been eying each other on the train but he hadn't made a move until they were outside the terminal and he was able to ditch his friend. She had been fantasizing about him for most of the trip so it was a shock to suddenly be together with him in the back of a cab hurtling into the night.

She was worried, and with good reason, that Veronica would make a play for her boyfriend when she was in town, and as a consequence she didn't encourage her to come home for the weekends.

"Keep trying to call her, OK?"

"If you talk to her tell her to call me."

"I'll tell her," Sara says. And then, after a pause: "If I remember."

As soon as he hangs up Harry dials Marina's number.

"I want to come over," he says.

"It's late. I have to get up tomorrow."

"I'll be over in an hour."

"And then what?"

"I'll leave in the morning."

He can still feel the sting of Sara's voice. He can't understand why she feels so angry at him. It was she who'd fooled around while they were married; now, typically, she's using her aggressiveness as a defense against something indefensible. What she could accuse him of—and this is the arrow he had to deflect over and over again during the last years of their marriage—was a kind of abandonment. Putting his job first over his family. Most of the cops he knows are on their second or third marriages or live alone.

And when he *was* home? Did they ever take a vacation? Did they ever travel anywhere?

For years, Sara had been trying to convince him to go to Italy, but it never happened. She and Veronica are tentatively thinking of going there together next summer. What were they doing now, she and the guy? Talking about him, no doubt, the guy asking questions, nervous about the idea that his lover's former husband is a cop. The image of them together is what gives Harry energy. He might have been content to just nod out in his own bed, but hearing the voice of Sara's boyfriend changes everything. The fact that he's jealous after all this time—a kind of internal bleeding that's familiar to him, it's like being home—was accompanied by a sense of amazement at his own vulnerability. It's like the wing of a terrifying prehistoric bird is hovering over him, and there's no way to escape. He feels like it's beneath his dignity to care about the way Sara lives her life, but for the length of the phone conversation—and its immediate aftermath—he feels a distinct absence of dignity or pride. It was still his apartment, Sara was still his wife. The lease was in his name. The telephone and utilities bills were in his name. The boyfriend was lying in his bed, the same one that Harry and Sara had bought together. Despite all these old ties, the only thing really binding them is their daughter. And sometimes Harry has the thought that even she no longer matters. Not as a link, anyway, though it's true if Veronica didn't exist he would have no contact with his former wife. Never call her number and hear the voice of a strange man.

The streets are empty Sunday night and it won't take long to get to Marina's apartment in Brighton Beach.

There were words which designated the things that he saw, but he didn't see anything really, not in the clear space of a reality in which his attention swooped down on something and surrounded it, absorbed it into his being, made it his own. Inanimate reality rarely allowed for that to happen, though many people had the power to will it into being. There was safety in objects, in relationships with the things of the world. People were more risky. People became disappointed in you. They fought back.

He takes the Bowery to the Manhattan Bridge, rolls down the window and holds the night air in his lungs. There are no other cars going in his direction except for a cab with an off-duty light turned on that eventually passes him on the incline at the bottom of the bridge, and a sign advertising *The Watchtower*, newspaper for a million Jehovah's Witnesses, looms in the right-hand corner of the windshield. Down Flatbush Avenue to Grand Army Plaza with its emblazoned statues commemorating the dead from some past war that's no longer relevant. There were faster ways of getting to the ocean but he likes this route best. He and Sara lived not far from here, a side street on the edge of Prospect Park, for a year after Veronica was born. They had spent weekend afternoons in late spring and summer sitting on a blanket in the park while Veronica slept in her stroller. Then they would take endless walks, past ball fields and gazebos and reflecting pools, past the Quaker Cemetery where famous movie stars like Montgomery Clift were buried. Sara had returned to school, something she'd always wanted to do; she hired a baby-sitter for the two evenings a week that she attended classes. Harry's absences weren't a problem. Often he'd return home late at night and she'd turn over in bed, half-asleep but still receptive, uncomplaining, glad to talk to him if that's what he wanted or have sex if he wanted that as well, even though with a one-year-old he knew she needed more sleep, that there were never enough hours in the day to take care of a child, go to school, and make someone else happy. In the morning he would wake to the smell of fresh coffee and Veronica would crawl into his bed and punch him in the shoulder and sit on his chest until he was fully awake.

 He drives through the night saying their names out the open window. *Sara. Veronica.* As if they were in the next room.

He can smell the ocean as he passes Avenue X. The streets are lettered, A to Z, on the way to the ocean.

He makes a mental note—"call Ricardo about porn film director"—but it would wait till tomorrow. The porn director had given him the name of a person who had been harassing Yvonne de Marco. A woman, no less, who thought Yvonne was sleeping with her boyfriend.

Marina lives on a side street a block from the el. A six-story nondescript red brick apartment building built in the 1960s on a street that was mostly two-family houses surrounded by wrought-iron fences with steps leading up to the front door. Harry circles the block a few times and finally parks in front of a meter on a street leading down to the ocean. He forgot to bring his jacket and wears only a black cashmere sweater (a birthday gift from Sara five years before) with a long-sleeved jersey beneath it, and he's cold, he hates the cold, the idea of winter up ahead, the chill beneath his skin as the wind batters the canopies of the restaurants on Brighton Avenue and a traffic light sways erratically above an intersection a half-block from Marina's apartment. He runs through the mist as thunder rolls over the boardwalk leading to Coney Island a half-mile away. He can see her windows from the street. Expects to see her leaning out, waiting for him in anticipation, but she isn't there.

He doesn't realize that he's taking her for granted in the same way he did with Sara, that he assumes she'll be there whenever he wants to see her, that she'll never say no to him or turn away from him in bed as Sara had done. For all he knows—and he would go crazy if he thought about it—she could be on the phone with her other boyfriend right now. He wonders if Judith told her that they spent an afternoon in bed, whether they talk about him at all. He had been waiting for some fallout, some repercussions. If he had known that she was Marina's friend it would never have happened, but that didn't excuse the fact that he had wanted it to happen regardless of what Marina thought. He had been careful not to go back to Yvonne de Marco's building for fear of seeing her again. He wanted to see her again. He and Ricardo had interviewed all the actors and directors of Yvonne de Marco's movies, all the men who had fucked her on screen, but there was still no motive why anyone would want to murder her. It wasn't that the people they talked to weren't capable of killing her; there was just no one with a real reason. Even the jealous wife, Harry thought, would turn into a dead end, and no one would say anything incriminating about anyone else. Ricardo held out hope for the possibility that it was someone in the building or neighborhood who had committed the murder.

He rings Marina's buzzer and she lets him in without asking him to identify himself.

He assured Ricardo that Judith had told them everything she knew, that it would be a waste of time to talk to her again, and he looked at Harry wide-eyed, as if his partner himself was concealing evidence that was crucial to solving the murder. As if he was covering up, lying to protect someone, though mostly Harry was worried that Judith would seduce his partner as well. ("If she slept with me," he thought, "she'll sleep with anyone.")

Marina's apartment is on the fifth floor. Instead of taking the elevator like he usually does, he climbs the stairs.

It's eleven o'clock. There was graffiti spray-painted on the wall of the stairwell. Shapes of letters that resemble Chinese characters. He pauses at each landing for ten seconds to catch his breath.

There was the moment, a few days ago, when he was in Judith's apartment and he realized that she wanted to have sex with him. That she knew why he had returned and that it had nothing to do with Yvonne de Marco. It was her look, the tilt of her head, that had made him feel naked, like she could read his mind. She put her finger to her lips as a sign that she knew what he was thinking. That he didn't have to say anything.

He knocks on Marina's door and she says "It's open" and he turns the knob.

From inside the apartment, she says "It's open" and he lets himself in.

They're on top of him immediately, pulling him downward from two sides. There's no time to protect himself. One of them smashes his face with the butt of a gun. The other twists his arm behind him, wrenching it from the socket.

"Does he have a piece?"

This is the third guy talking from across the room.

Harry, his eyes like splintered glass, can see Marina huddled in the doorway of the living room. Smoking a cigarette. Just a blur against the spiral of light and shadow, the beam of a flashlight disappearing in the fog. What he's feeling is beyond pain, somewhere out of reach, as his awareness of the shapes and forms around him begin to fade, along with the shape of his own thoughts, which have been reduced to a series of single words or names, as if he's calling for help and no one can hear, or simply saying goodbye.

"I'm sorry," Marina says, and the guy standing next to her slaps her face.

They have his gun. Two bald Russian men with double chins and coarse skin are standing over him. They take turns kicking him in the chest and groin. They're talking in Russian. Ivan, the bearded guy standing next to Marina, says: "Take him into the other room," and one of the bald guys says, "He's a cop. Boris isn't going to be happy about this."

Ivan laughs. "Boris can take care of the cops. That's what he does best."

Harry's lying on the floor and Ivan kicks him in the head for good measure.

"What about her?" one of the guys says.

"My business," Ivan says. He reaches out to stroke Marina's hair but she pulls away from him.

The two men drag Harry's body across the gray carpet, maneuvering it down the hallway leading to the bedroom.

A sudden gust of rain sprays against the living room windows. It's the storm coming up over the ocean, the tail of a hurricane that's created disaster areas up and down the southern coast.

Key West, where Harry and Sara spent their honeymoon, has been evacuated. Marina can feel Ivan's breath on the side of her neck.

"I love you," he says, in English, hissing in her ear. "When I was in prison...." His thoughts trail off. Why is he bothering?

He takes a knife from his pocket, presses a button on the handle.

It was a special knife, a gift from Slater, a man he had met in prison. All the time in prison he was known as "Slater's Woman." If Slater hadn't protected him, he would never have survived.

Slater even made Ivan dress like a woman. He was having sex with one of the guards in exchange for cigarettes, chocolate, and clothing. He would wrap the gifts in old newspaper and present them to Ivan. Slater liked the touch of silk against his skin. In the darkness, you could pretend you were making love to anyone.

The two Russian guys reappear in the living room and stare disapprovingly at the scene.

"I thought you were going to kill her," one of them says.

"I will," Ivan says. "No one tells me what to do."

"Boris tells us. He says your girlfriend is sleeping

with a cop. Too dangerous. Kill them both."

"He says, 'Kill them both,' that's what we do."

"And now the cops are going to think you did it."

They had forgotten about Marina. She takes the gun from the pocket of her skirt—Harry had given it to her a few days before, overriding her insistence that she didn't need it—and shoots both of the Russian men in the face. Their bodies slide backwards against the wall in slow motion, like out-of-shape athletes unwinding against the side of a fence after a bad game. Instead of sweat, rivulets of blood pour down their chins. Their eyes are wide open but only the whites are showing.

Then she points the gun at Ivan.

"This is for Irene," she says, but she isn't sure why. Nothing she can do will bring Irene back.

As he comes towards her, slicing the air with the blade, she closes her eyes and squeezes the trigger with both hands, the way Harry taught her.

The shot hits him in the chest, right below the heart. He drops the knife and falls to his knees. Blood bubbles at the corners of his mouth and spreads like a spider web down the front of his shirt.

"And this one," she says, pressing the gun against the side of his head, "is for me."

When one has had a dream one can tell it to another person, but this which she had to tell was no dream, it was real, and yet when she wished to speak of it and relieve her troubled mind, there was nothing to tell.

Kierkegaard

LEWIS WARSH is the author of over thirty volumes of poetry, fiction and autobiography, including *Out of the Question: Selected Poems 1963-2003* (Station Hill, 2017), *Alien Abduction* (Ugly Duckling Presse, 2015), *One Foot Out the Door: Collected Stories* (Spuyten Duyvil, 2014), *A Place in the Sun* (Spuyten Duyvil, 2010) and *Inseparable: Poems 1995-2005* (Granary Books, 2008). He was co-founder, with Bernadette Mayer, of *United Artists* Magazine and Books. He has received grants from the National Endowment for the Arts, the New York State Council of the Arts, The Poet's Foundation and The Fund for Poetry. *Mimeo Mimeo #7* (2012) was devoted to his poetry, fiction and collages, and to a bibliography of his work as a writer and publisher. He has taught at Naropa University, The Poetry Project, SUNY Albany, Bowery Poetry and Long Island University, where he was director of the MFA program in creative writing from 2007-2013 and where he currently teaches.

www.ingramcontent.com/pod-product-compliance
Lightning Source LLC
LaVergne TN
LVHW040140080526
838202LV00042B/2965